Beyond The Garden Wall

Patsy Collins

Contents

1. Tackling The Wisteria

"Anything in particular you'd like to do today?" my husband Geoff asked as he brought me an early morning cup of tea.

"I thought we could tackle the wisteria."

"Today?"

"Yes. Unless the weather forecast is bad?" It wouldn't be sensible to be at the top of a ladder, secateurs in hand, reaching for wayward shoots if it were windy. And it would be no fun at all in the rain.

"No, it looks set to be a lovely day. I'm just surprised you'd want to do something so much like a job of work on your first day of retirement."

Although I'd worked in an office, and gardening was my passion, I knew what he meant. The wisteria was huge. My grandparents planted it when they moved in, before my dad was born. It doesn't just cover the entire front of our house, but that of the neighbours' too. And our garage. And theirs. Pruning it, although worthwhile and very satisfying when done, was hard work. It was possible in a single day, if we started early, were disciplined about taking only the shortest of breaks and put all our energy into it. And had plenty of Radox ready for a much needed soak afterwards!

"It does need doing," I pointed out. The previous year, due to lack of time, it had only had a quick trim to stop it blocking windows, which is why I'd now referred to 'tackling' rather than pruning the thing. "And this is the right time of year."

"Yes, but I thought we might do something more fun today. Make a kind of celebration of it."

"We spent all last week celebrating my retirement." That's a slight exaggeration, but I'd worked in the same school all my working life so staff and pupils, past and present, had made something of a fuss of me. And my husband, children and grandchildren had too. Our family doesn't waste any opportunity to get together and eat a lot of cake!

"We will do the wisteria, and soon, but we've got all the time in the world for things like that."

"Yes, I know." It was a thought I'd been trying to push out of my head.

"Do you have something in mind?" I asked.

"I do actually." He did of course. Since he'd retired, four months previously, he'd completed lots of jobs that had been put off until we had time. He'd have done the wisteria already if that wasn't a two person task. He'd been waiting for me to stop working, so we could start doing the fun things together.

"Does it involve cake?"

His grin answered that one.

"Count me in," I said.

On the way to the first place, he promised we'd do the wisteria the following day. "Sorry, I hadn't realised it was bothering you that much. I'd have had a go if I had. Phil next door would have held the ladder for me."

"I'm not that bothered."

"You sounded like you were."

"OK, I was bothered, but not by the wisteria. It was what you said about having all the time in the world."

"Isn't that a good thing?"

"In theory, but it reminded me of my grandparents, my gran in particular. Whenever I went round there or phoned up it was often because I wanted something – I didn't mean to be like that and have only just realised I was."

"It's typical of the young, I think. It's not selfishness exactly, they just think of the world as revolving around them. Our kids were like that for a while and the grandkids haven't quite grown out of it."

"Yes, I think that's what it was. I did at least ask if I was interrupting anything and they always said no, they had all the time in the world for me."

"I don't quite see the problem. I remember your gran and she adored you." He reminded me that visits would have meant my grandparents stopping what they were doing and having tea and cake. I didn't need to feel guilty for giving them an excuse to do that.

"You're right. I don't feel guilty. Thanks, love." Guilt wasn't what was bothering me, but I put it aside to enjoy our day.

We had a lovely time looking round two wonderful gardens, investing in their plant shops and eating in the tearooms of the second one. Afterwards we visited a place which sold reclaimed and antique garden items. We'd promised ourselves a water feature and hoped to find something suitable. The old barrel and hand operated pump were perfect. We'd walked a few miles and were on our feet for a good eight hours, but none of it was what you'd call work. The new plants we bought would need planting and the water feature required us to find a suitable location, clear it, and assemble the thing. Those were the kind of tasks we most enjoyed. They involved a lot of walking round the garden thinking and planning. Lots of sitting down with tea and cake and thinking and planning. And the work, once we started, could be done in stages. With tea breaks in between, or stopping to tie in the clematis which we'd suddenly noticed had shot up, or a nice long chat with someone who'd rung up or called round unexpectedly.

That night I tried to explain to Geoff why being reminded of my grandparents had bothered me. "It was because they'd seemed to have no life of their own after retirement. Gran had worked in the post office and told me enough about it for me to know it was a responsible position, involving a lot more than selling stamps and weighing parcels. Grandad had an important role in the local factory which at the time employed more than half the town's population."

"Your job at the school was a responsible post too and you must know you were important to a lot of people. Look how many came to your retirement events."

"That's part of it. When working I was like them and I'm worried I will be in retirement too."

"You think they weren't happy?"

"I thought they were, but now I look back it seems almost as though they did nothing but sit around waiting for me to turn up, or call for advice or to complain how unfair life was. At the time I'd taken it for granted they always had time for me, but now I'm dreading having a life where the only interest is contact with my grandchildren."

Don't get me wrong, I absolutely love them, we both do. One of the positives of retirement was that we could have them to stay for weeks at a time in the holidays, we'd be able to attend every play and sport's day. I just didn't want that to be our entire lives.

"I see what you mean, but think you're worrying for nothing. We've got holidays planned, you're starting that poetry course next month, there's the garden…"

"I know. You're right." He almost had me convinced.

"Wisteria today then?" Geoff asked as he brought me in an early morning cup of tea the next morning.

"Yes. Oh gosh, you should have woken me earlier! We won't get it all done today."

"We don't have to. All the time in the world, remember? I've been thinking… We should have a proper breakfast first and get the ladder set up and everything ready, have a tea break, then do the cutting of just one section. The neighbours are at work so we can start that side. Do their garage today and the house tomorrow. We needn't do the picking up and tying back until after lunch, as the detritus and ladder won't be in their way."

"Good plan. It will take longer, but it will be less stressful – not to mention more sensible not to be working hard without decent meal breaks."

We did exactly that. As usual my husband went up the ladder to do the cutting, with me steadying it and calling advice about which bits to cut and which to leave to tie in to extend the ancient plant's reach. For the second stage we swapped roles. I did the tying in, while he held the ladder straight and directed me to do the same with the stems. It was fortunate that, although since my grandparents had bought the semi-detached house there had been several changes of neighbours, all had been happy to have the plant trail over their property as long as they could enjoy the wonderful scented blooms without having to do the work required to keep it out of gutters, away from window frames and blooming profusely.

Doing the first section of the plant didn't take all day, despite our tea and lunch break.

"Shall we start the next bit?" I suggested.

"No. We won't have time to clear it all up before the neighbours get back. I don't suppose they'd mind, but as we haven't warned them it would be a shock."

He had a point. We decided to just remove all the bits we'd cut off and pile them up in our garden, to deal with at the end. A good decision, leaving us time to walk round our garden and decide on the ideal spot for our new water feature.

Four days later we'd cut back every wayward wisteria shoot, tied in every stem, and removed every trace of our activities. Well not removed – moved to a hug pile in our garden.

"I'm looking forward to getting rid of that," I said, "but as we'll need to cut back the laurel for the water feature, maybe we should do that first?"

"Good idea, then we can shred the whole lot at once."

We cut a fair bit off the laurel bush. Then quite a lot more.

"Do you actually like this?" Geoff asked.

"Not especially. It's good to have something to look at here as we can see it from the kitchen window…"

"But we won't need it now we've got the water feature?"

"Exactly."

Getting it out was a terrific job. At one point we decided we'd wait for Phil next door to come home and add a bit more muscle to our attempts to pull up the root. After a refreshing cup of tea and fortifying wedge of cake, Geoff thought of sawing through the root while it was still in the ground.

"Worth a try," I agreed.

The saw was fit for the bin, and we were in need of more cake when we'd finished, but we got it out in the end.

"Hello!" a voice called. Our granddaughter Kate.

"Out in the garden love, come round."

She did. "Oh, you got rid of a bush!" Kate had only noticed we'd removed the laurel because the remains of it were lying on the lawn. She couldn't see the effort it had taken, just as she hadn't realised the front of our house looked tidy again because we'd spent four days up ladders pruning the wisteria.

"Yes, we're going to put a water feature here," Geoff explained.

"Nice."

Kate didn't see the fun we'd had choosing it, the time we'd spend assembling it, the trips we'd make to get ideas for planting around it, the way we'd messed about pumping the handle over enthusiastically so we splashed each other.

"Are you busy now?" Kate asked. "Only I wanted to ask your advice about something."

Just as when I was her age, her mind was on herself and her reason for being there. She didn't see our lives were full even when she left, simply because she was young.

"No love, we're not too busy for that," Geoff said.

"Let's go in and put the kettle on," I added. We had a mountain of shredding to do, the stump and roots of the laurel to take to the tip, the water feature to assemble… but all that could wait. "We have all the time in the world to talk to you, Kate my love."

2. The Committee's Decision

"Next up on the agenda is Antonia Blossom's B&B. Do we grant her the Norton-on-Sea Traditional Hospitality Rosette?" the chairman asked.

"Absolutely not!" was the opinion of Muriel Bainbridge, proprietor of the Sea View guest house and holder of a bronze rosette. "From what I've seen there's very little that's traditional about her place. It's very plain. All the clocks show different times. She uses plastic tablecloths and floor mats. The garden is… not to my taste shall we say? Weeds grow in the lawn and there's not a begonia or marigold in sight. Instead of a nice ornamental pond she's got little sheds that are no use to anyone and she serves the strangest food!"

Muriel's face was almost puce by the time she'd completed her uncharacteristic outburst. It clashed rather unfortunately with the pink iced French fancies which had been her contribution to the refreshments. These had been arranged, in a generous pyramid, onto a doily covered, willow pattern plate.

Muriel's place was traditional all right, and nobody could describe it as plain. Knitted ladies adorned the spare toilet rolls on every avocado green cistern. Every bed had a multi-coloured crocheted throw, every light a frilled shade. Every wall, carpet, sofa and tablecloth sported a different pattern. Everywhere you looked was floral and flock, chintz and tartan, Paisley and gingham, houndstooth and polka dots, stripes, swirls or geometric art deco. There were china ducks in flight over one lounge wall, while Constable's

Haywain hung opposite. Porcelain shepherdesses and cute china dogs graced the plentiful shelves. Unlike Antonia's establishment, at Muriel's there wasn't a scrap of plastic or undecorated space in the entire building. It was all very popular with Americans who thought it 'quaint' and took plenty of photographs to show friends back home.

The landlord of the Royal Oak, holder of a gold rosette, spoke next. "Antonia's place isn't traditionally decorated, but she's certainly hospitable. She's almost always full, even out of season and has many repeat visitors." She also advised them to have their dinner in the Royal Oak and occasionally popped in for a drink herself. The landlord helped himself from the platter of roast beef sandwiches he'd brought.

"She doesn't seem to be against traditional seaside entertainment," said the owner of the crazy golf course. The decision on his rosette was awaiting completion of the tea room he was having built. He'd supplied the tea for the meeting and offered to do all the washing up. "Lots of her guests come down to me on her recommendation and she always tells them how well stocked the local shops are."

Various shopkeepers acknowledged this, and spoke in Antonia's favour.

"She's public spirited too," the vicar added. "She always volunteers a raffle prize for our fundraising events." He gave pointed looks at those amongst the committee who sometimes had to be prompted into being equally obliging.

"And her unusual donations are often the first things to go," pointed out the director of the local theatre. He should know as he often tried to win them as props. Antonia always displayed his posters and was responsible for a large proportion of ticket sales. She organised the refreshments too, which greatly assisted the theatre gain its silver rosette.

"I'm not saying she's a bad person," Muriel said. "She certainly isn't. I only know what her place is like because she let me stay there when I'd accidentally overbooked and had to give up my own room. Actually that was extremely generous of her; anyone else would have taken the extra paying guests instead." Muriel's blush deepened. "But the rosettes are for traditional hospitality, not niceness."

There was a lull in the conversation as everyone digested the truth of Muriel's words and consumed the rest of the tempting tea laid out before them.

The chairman cleared his throat. "I think we need an independent assessment. My cousin and her family are visiting soon. I'll ask them to stay at Antonia's anonymously and see what the place is like from a guest's point of view."

A month later the committee met again to talk and eat. The chairman gave his cousin's feedback. "Everything is as Muriel observed during her brief stay, well almost. The clocks *are* set at different times, but there's a note by each saying if it's UK time, or European or Canadian."

"I did see signs," Muriel admitted. "I only slept there and had to rush back to my guests first thing each morning, so didn't have time to read them or ask questions. Do you know why she does it?"

"Apparently guests frequently asked what the time was in different countries so they knew when to call home. There's a reason for the plastic tablecloths and floor-mats too. They're used in a special area for small children. My cousin said knowing that, if they made a mess it didn't matter too much, helped her relax. In other places they've stayed she's felt bad when the children dropped something and tried to clean it before the landlady noticed."

"Oh." Muriel rarely had guests under the age of fifty. "Well, what about her strange sheds?"

"They're mini beach huts for pets; anything from guinea pigs to donkeys. She also has an area reserved to let dogs and other creatures out for a run."

"That'll be the reason for the weeds, I suppose," Muriel suggested.

"Actually I think what you saw was the wildflower meadow. Instead of bedding displays her garden is full of our native plants, butterflies and birds. And as for the strange food, that's perhaps explained by the fact that she's delighted to cater for those with special dietary needs. Whether you're vegan, lactose intolerant, diabetic or have strange pregnancy cravings, Antonia will serve you the perfect breakfast."

"Even so," Muriel said, "I stand by my view that her place isn't a traditional seaside guest house and therefore she shouldn't be awarded a Norton-on-Sea Traditional Hospitality Rosette."

Reluctantly the others agreed she had a valid point. Quietly they nibbled sandwiches and cake and sipped at their tea.

Muriel continued, "I propose we create a new category, that of individual welcome, and award Antonia a rosette. A gold one."

The proposal was accepted unanimously.

3. Fitting Tribute

Davie hesitated outside the florist shop. He and Maggie had agreed to buy a wreath spelling out 'Mum' but he had another idea he thought, hoped, would be a more fitting tribute to his mother-in-law. He also hoped that despite her grief it might put a smile on his wife's face. Davie too missed his mother-in-law enormously, but was trying to obey her wish of being remembered with the happiness she'd enjoyed throughout her ninety-three years. He remembered her too with gratitude.

Davie once attended a beginner's pottery club, where he'd made mugs. His first attempt was rather clumsy, but his own mother would like it because he'd made it and it was decorated in fiery red with 'Mum' picked out in rich orange – her favourite colours. His second mug was much neater and glazed in brilliant cobalt blue. 'Skylar' was marked with dozens of tiny stars, so he knew his sister would love it. The next was abnormally large, deliberately so. It was an attempt at slipware intended as a gift for his cousin Kiim. He and Skylar often jokingly consoled each other over never getting novelty gifts with their names on.

Some club members wanted to sell their work at a craft fair. Davie agreed his mugs could go on the stall to bulk out the display. In the unlikely event someone bought one he'd make another, which due to his increasing skill would likely be better than the original.

Davie was flattered that several people admired his efforts. "It's nice to see something a bit different, not the kind of thing you can buy anywhere," people said. Or,

"Lovely colours," or "That's how much coffee I need to wake me up in the morning."

One gorgeous girl asked, "Do you take orders? My mum's name is unusual and I'd love to surprise her with something that has it on."

"You can have anything you like on it." He'd have done anything to make her smile, even back then. "What's your mum's name?"

"Alejandrina-Maria."

"You're joking?"

"Sorry, no. Well, I was joking about the mug. Of course you can't fit all that on, but it really is her name. Can I buy the Mum one?"

"No." If he sold her that she'd leave and he wouldn't see her again. "I'll make something special for you. Give me that name again." He wrote it down, and Maggie's number so he could contact her when it was ready.

"Any particular colour scheme?"

"Rainbow!"

Davie tried painting the name onto a mug, but making the letters small enough meant they were unreadable. Instead he made a long thin rainbow plate – just wide enough for a single biscuit and long enough for the whole packet or all the letters of Maggie's mum's name. Davie also made a set of six mugs in different colours, with part of the name on each.

"These are absolutely fantastic!" Maggie said when she saw them. "I can't thank you enough. What do I owe you?"

He'd not even thought about setting a price and in any case her smile was reward enough. "How about you thank me by coming out with me one night? That's if you're single and want to of course… No pressure and you're welcome to the mugs and plate anyway."

She'd given him that lovely smile. "As it happens I am currently single, and if that's the only way you'll let me pay, I'll buy you dinner."

Davie let himself be persuaded and had taken no convincing that their date should happen that same evening.

"Mum is thrilled with the biscuit plate and absolutely loves her mugs," Maggie told him once they'd ordered. "She says her name will only be whole when she has friends and family round to share food and drink and that's just how she feels about herself."

"I like the sound of her," Davie said.

"That's not what you said when I told you her name!"

"You know what I mean."

Maggie agreed she did. And the next day she called him to say, "Mum likes the sound of you too, and wants you to come round to drink from one of the mugs."

Of course he'd accepted that invitation and many more. Alejandrina-Maria's large circle of family and friends put in orders for more of Davie's hand made items, often wanting uncommon names on them or asking for non standard shapes or sizes. Sets of mugs, each with just a few letters spelling out names or messages when assembled together were especially popular. The money Davie made enabled him to buy a small home kiln, so he was able to produce more pieces than he could by using the club's, whenever space was available.

Maggie suggested selling some at craft fairs. "It would be fun going to those on a weekend."

Davie had liked the idea, but his items sold as fast as he could make them, so he never built up a stock. A few months later he was engaged to Maggie and regularly refusing pottery orders as he simply couldn't keep up with demand.

"I wish I could do this full time," he told Alejandrina-Maria when he agreed to make a cake plate to match her mugs, but warned there would be a long wait.

"Then why don't you? Maggie could help and you'd be together doing something you both enjoy, rather than apart doing jobs which are no fun."

"You're right, but I'd need a bigger kiln. I can't afford to buy one and give up work at the same time. I wouldn't get a loan. I'm sure I could make it work, but convincing a bank is another matter."

"Sounds as though you've already considered this."

Davie admitted it.

"How much would you need? Absolute minimum?"

"Three thousand pounds."

"That's your wedding present sorted then."

It wasn't just the money which was such a massive support to Davie in setting up his specialist pottery business, but Alejandrina-Maria's faith in him that providing it demonstrated. That gave him the confidence he needed to go ahead. She'd helped with selling and advertising, taking turns on the stall and putting leaflets through doors. At first she did that alone, in place of the pregnant Maggie, later taking the children with her.

Alejandrina-Maria's treatment of Davie wasn't anything special by her standards. She was just as generous with her love, time and even money when needed with everyone she cared about and there were many, many such people.

Now they'd lost her and had to buy a wreath for her funeral. Davie and Maggie had agreed on 'Mum' in white carnations. He wasn't quite sure how they'd decided on that – there had been so many decisions which neither of them had wanted to make, but couldn't avoid. There were many others who wanted to pay tribute. Maggie and Davie suggested simple bunches of carnations or gerberas in bright colours – exactly the sort of thing people used to bring when they visited her and which she'd always appreciated. That seemed fitting. The plain wreath didn't.

Davie squeezed Maggie's hand, pushed open the door to the florist shop and led her inside. She was too upset to speak, so he explained why they were there.

"Ah yes. I have your order here. White carnations, that's right?"

Davie glanced at the paperwork. "Yes, but instead of Mum could we have her name?"

"You can have anything you like. What is, was, her name?"

"Alejandrina-Maria."

"You're joking. Oh! I'm so sorry."

"What did you say?" Maggie asked.

"I'm sorry, I was just surprised. I'm so sorry if I caused offence."

"You didn't. You just reminded me of something. So can you do it, a wreath with her whole name on?"

"Yes. Well, not strictly one wreath. It would have to be in sections, but it would look like one when put together."

"That would be an awful lot of white carnations," Davie said.

"No problem. We can easily order them in."

Maggie looked up at him. "Are you thinking what I'm thinking?"

He hoped so. "Not all white, and not all from us?"

"Exactly."

"Could we have a think and confirm the order tomorrow?" Davie asked the florist.

"If it's before noon I'll be able to order whatever's needed in time."

"I'll call first thing."

A meeting of family and close friends had been organised for that evening, to decide on the songs to play at Mum's celebration of life. Davie told them his idea.

When Alejandrina-Maria was laid to rest the floral tribute was her name spelled out in a multitude of flowers and colours, those for the various letters selected by different friends and family members. Together it looked like one single, joyful arrangement.

"This is perfect," Maggie whispered. "Just as having family and friends around completed Mum's mug set and made her feel whole, this brings us all together to remember her. While we have each other, we haven't quite lost her." Tears dripped down Maggie's face, but she was smiling too.

4. Haring About

I ran up Mike's path and banged on the door. And rang the bell. And shouted.

It seemed ages before he wrenched it open, but as I was still gasping for breath, maybe it wasn't.

"What on earth… Oh. Hello, Chloe. For a moment there I thought something serious had happened."

"It has. Beryl's tortoise has escaped!"

He actually laughed.

"This is not funny, Mike! She's going in to have her second cataract operation this afternoon and if she's worried about him it's not going to help. You've always been annoying, but I didn't realise you were too heartless to help a sweet old lady."

"Chloe, calm down," he interrupted. "I was only laughing at the sight of someone red-faced and sweaty in pursuit of a tortoise. Of course I don't want Beryl worried and will come and help look."

Of course he would. That's why I'd gone straight to him the moment I realised I needed help to find the creature. Maybe his motives are sometimes kind and generous, I'm not the best person to judge him on that, but his actions often seem so. Whatever he does, Mike always manages to make himself look good.

Just to prove I'm not the sort to hold a grudge or anything, I'll admit he looks very, very good. As he was in shorts and T-shirt showing off tanned and toned muscles, maybe it was a good thing I had an excuse for being a little bit hot and bothered. Really though, I only noticed the kissably soft skin of his throat because I'd caught a glimpse of the gold chain around his neck. Was there any significance to the fact he still wore a gift from me?

We searched Mike's garden. Or rather I did as he followed me round asking stupid questions such as how long Beryl had owned a tortoise, why she'd decided to get one, where she kept it and what it looked like. Don't know if I told you he was annoying, but if not you've probably worked that out yourself.

"I have no idea," I said in answer to his questions. Actually I may have snapped. I wasn't worried about the animal, if anything bad had happened to it we'd probably have heard, but I didn't want Beryl getting anxious about it. "Don't they all look the same?" I asked. "If we find a tortoise which doesn't belong to the garden's owner then the chances are that it will be Beryl's."

He didn't look exactly convinced, but suggested we split up. Again! But like I said, I don't hold grudges and can actually barely remember those couple of dates when I was fourteen. Nor the fiasco in the Red Swan when I was nineteen which might possibly have been my fault. As for the row earlier in the year, which definitely had been, I was doing my absolute best to forget about that.

"Chloe?" Mike lightly touched my shoulder.

"Sorry, what did you say?"

Mike suggested I continue down Mulberry Road, where Beryl, Mike and my aunt all live, whilst he tried Cherry Drive. The houses of that street backed onto those in Mulberry Road, so Mike's suggestion made sense. Which is more than can be said for of all of his neighbours.

Between the lot of them they asked the same stupid questions as Mike had, several different times. "How long has Beryl owned a tortoise?" "Why did she decide to get one?" "Where does she keep it?" "What does it look like?" At least they all knew about Beryl's imminent visit to hospital, so I didn't have to explain the urgency of the search. It wasn't until I'd crawled under three hedges, squeezed behind four sheds and been scratched by a dozen different bushes that I started to wonder the same things and to think back.

"Can I persuade you to do a week's housesitting?" my aunt and godmother said about six weeks ago. Just to clarify, my aunt is my godmother; I didn't have two different women making the same request in unison. I'm explaining that because it confuses some people and I've been accused of making things complicated, jumping to the wrong conclusions, creating chaos and dragging others along with me. These days I'm not like that at all. Not that I ever was, obviously. OK, I was a bit, but I really have learned my lesson.

"Is the housesitting for you?" I asked. See, no jumping to conclusions or agreeing before I had the facts and so making life overly complicated.

"Sort of. I want you to stay in my house, but it's really my neighbour Beryl I want you to keep an eye on." She explained that Beryl's second cataract operation was due the same week as her holiday. "I offered to cancel, but she wouldn't hear of it. She says she'll only be in the hospital a couple of hours and it's a common and simple procedure, which she's been through before."

Knowing Beryl has no close relations I asked, "Do you want me to take her in and pick her up?"

"Actually it's before she goes in that concerns me. When she had the first one she was a bit nervous. She says she isn't this time, but if I was there I'd pop in for chats and give her the chance to talk through any concerns. That's what I'd like you to do."

"That makes sense, but I don't know much about cataract surgery."

"Beryl does. After the first one she told me how quick and painless it was, that the result was wonderful and how she needn't have worried. You could get her to talk about it and remind herself of those facts."

"And that's all?" Beryl is a delight and the road where she and my godmother live is mainly occupied by pleasant, neighbourly people – I didn't think Beryl would be short of someone to talk to.

"That's all. Mike is taking her to the hospital and bringing her home. And another neighbour is going to stay with her the first night – longer if she needs it."

It was the mention of Mike which convinced me to accept. I had no wish to see him myself naturally, but I couldn't in all conscience leave Beryl with only such an unsympathetic person to look after her.

Remembering that, just as I was exploring the muddy depths of number 27's fishpond made my face flush again. I had been just a tiny bit hasty and unfair in accusing Mike of being unwilling to help his neighbour. He'd had to take the day off work to do the hospital runs, but then Beryl is lovely; anyone would want to help her. It has nothing to do with him being a nice person, although just conceivably he is to some people.

When I was seven he'd found a grass snake and terrorised me with it in my godmother's garden. Beryl rescued me.

After a cup of sweet tea and slice of lemon drizzle cake I'd begun to feel silly for over-reacting and behaving like such a wimp. Beryl had comforted me, saying it was perfectly natural to be alarmed by the snake. She herself had a horror of anything scaly.

Beryl has always been a very feminine woman. She is always perfectly made up and often wears a jingly charm bracelet and pretty brooches. There's a lot of pink frilliness in her home, which she keeps neat. The same goes for her garden. Multi-petalled pink flowers fill every available bit of space. There's nothing as utilitarian as a shed, and her dustbin is hidden away behind trellis smothered in roses.

Why would a woman like that own a tortoise? When had she acquired it? Where did she keep it and what did it look like? It wasn't the owner of the next house along asking me those questions. I was wondering that myself. What the homeowner said was, "A tortoise? Beryl? Are you sure?"

I certainly had been, but by then it was seeming more and more unlikely. Beryl had all her marbles and wasn't the sort to lie or play a silly joke. Mike though… No, although I wouldn't put it past him to get me on an imaginary tortoise hunt for a laugh, he hadn't been the person who'd started me looking. I'd done that myself. Could I have made things complicated, jumped to the wrong conclusions, created chaos and dragged others along with me? Realising it was just possible, I decided I should rule that out, by getting as many facts as possible and stopping to think, before taking further action.

I went back to Beryl's house, intending to ask how long she'd owned a tortoise, why she'd decided to get one, where she kept it and what it looked like. Mike arrived just as I did. For once, he seemed to be the one at a disadvantage. He was scratched, red-faced and sweaty.

Beryl peered at him, then asked him to step closer. She ushered him into the kitchen. We dabbed antiseptic onto his injuries and pulled leaves out of his hair.

"What on earth has happened to you, Mike?" Beryl asked.

"I've been looking for your tortoise in Cherry Drive," he explained.

"Why would you go all round there? It will be in the house somewhere. Don't worry about it though, I'll have no trouble seeing it once my other eye is fixed."

Lost, that's what she'd said, not escaped. Finally I asked the right question. "What exactly does it look like?"

"Small and silver, obviously."

"Obviously," Mike said.

I glanced at Beryl's charm bracelet with its tiny silver birds, flowers, lucky symbols and animals. "Oh."

"Perhaps you should leave the bracelet here while you're in hospital, in case any of the other charms are loose?" Mike suggested.

"Good idea." She took it off and handed it to me. "Would you put it in my jewellery box, Chloe love? It's on my dressing table."

By the time I got back downstairs, Mike had gone to change and bring his car round, ready to drive Beryl to hospital. I went in with them.

We sat outside in the sun as Beryl had her surgery. While we waited, I apologised for making things complicated, jumping to the wrong conclusions, creating chaos and dragging others along with me.

"Apology accepted," Mike said.

"I don't just mean about the tortoise," I told him.

"Neither do I. Do you have plans for the rest of the day?"

"Hunting in your garden for a small piece of precious metal."

"Beryl said the charm would be in her house," Mike reminded me.

"I know."

"So the thing you'll be looking for is…?"

"My engagement ring. I'm sorry I made such complicated plans for our wedding and dragged everyone along with the madness and I'm sorry I jumped to totally the wrong conclusion when you didn't think it was worth all the hassle and said we should take a break."

"I only meant that it wasn't worth getting upset if the hotel couldn't guarantee to find napkins the exact same shade as the invitations and just wanted a break from all the planning, not from you."

"I know that… now."

"So you forgive me?"

"There's nothing to forgive. You were right, Mike. I just wanted it to be perfect and got carried away as usual and ruined everything."

Except, perhaps that last bit wasn't entirely true? I'd thrown the ring at Mike and said I never wanted to see him again. Despite that he'd sent me roses on Valentine's Day and a first edition of my favourite book for my birthday. He'd cancelled the booking for our over the top reception, but not the service itself.

"Mike, I remember exactly where I was standing when I… when I took my ring off. Maybe we can find it?"

Mike hooked his finger under the neck of his T-shirt and pulled out the gold chain I'd given him for his twenty-first birthday. My engagement ring was threaded onto it.

I reached around his neck, intending to unclasp his chain and retrieve my ring. Maybe Mike jumped to conclusions or perhaps he just saw an opportunity. Either way, he pulled me closer and kissed me. I quickly realised that was a much better and simpler way to show how I felt, so joined in.

"Well now, that really is a sight for my not very sore eye!" Beryl said, when we went, hand in hand, to collect her.

5. Home At Last

Mandy didn't mind living in the flat. Young couples setting up a business don't have money for houses with gardens; they were lucky the space over their shop was a decent size and just about habitable. Their wedding presents helped a lot with that. As well as gifts of furnishings they were given offers of help with decorating, sewing, even carpentry.

"It looks so much better I hardly recognise the place," she'd said when they'd unwrapped and positioned the gifts and cashed in the work offers.

"I'm sorry it's not what you're used to," Leo replied. "I promise it's only temporary."

She'd done her best to explain that although her dad's rank in the army meant they'd always lived in nice houses, those too had always been temporary, so it was what she was used to.

"You know what I mean," Leo said.

Mandy did. Mum hadn't cooked on what was little more than a large camping stove, as she'd always had a proper hob and oven. She hadn't needed to go down the laundrette to wash and dry their clothes, as she'd always had a machine and somewhere to hang wet laundry. That outside space had usually been a lot prettier than a customer car park too. The unsettling feeling of impermanence was exactly the same though.

Mandy grew up constantly on the move. Maybe it wouldn't have troubled her had they not stayed put for three years from when she was eight. They'd had a wonderful garden in that particular house, with a huge apple tree. Dad had made a simple swing which she'd loved. Mandy had climbed into the tree, and put up a huge umbrella which she called a tree house. She'd watched the leaves sprout in spring, delighted in the plentiful but short-lived blossom, seen the fruits swell, then redden. Smelled them giving out the sweet fragrance which told her they were ready to eat, and kicked through its falling leaves for three years.

In the fourth year they'd moved on when the apples were still hard and green. They'd timed the move for the school holidays to provide as little disruption as possible. Mandy had of course known she was to move again. Knew she'd say goodbye to friends again.

"It'll be a new school for everyone in your year," Mum pointed out.

That was true but everyone else would know at least a few other people. They'd get there via familiar streets and return to a familiar house. Mandy had to start all over again.

Even worse was the loss of the tree. Had she given it a moment's thought she'd have realised it couldn't come with them, but somehow she'd assumed it would remain part of her life. When Dad realised she was upset about it he put up a swing in their new garden, and each garden afterwards if there was a suitable tree. In each he planted an apple tree. It pleased her to know that in the future many others would enjoy the blossom and fruit, but it wasn't the same as having a tree herself to enjoy in the present. Although Mandy did her best to be happy wherever she lived, and succeeded pretty well, she wouldn't let any new house take on the status of home in her heart.

The flat above their shop was better than all those houses because she didn't mind that she wouldn't live there forever.

If, or rather when, they moved it would be for somewhere better, not just somewhere else. The relocation wouldn't be something done to her, but a joint decision by herself and Leo. Maybe, if everything went perfectly, they'd find a real home.

They stayed in the flat a long time. Leo often went to the estate agency three doors down to enquire about suitable properties. Mandy never did. Leo took her several times to look at houses, but nowhere seemed right.

"We're so used to not travelling to work that a commute would be a step backwards," she said.

He agreed. After that, each prospective property was within walking distance of the shop. Some were nice, but none were quite right, so they'd still been in the flat on their fifth wedding anniversary, and sixth. And when Mandy fell pregnant.

"We really do have to move now, love," Leo said. "I wanted to before, but now I think you were right to wait. We can get somewhere perfect."

They could, if there was such a place. The period when Mandy lived in the house with the big apple tree had been idyllic. The summers were warm and dry, that particular job meant Dad was home every night, Mandy had good friends. Life was wonderful. But she'd been a child with no responsibilities and perhaps the way it was ripped away from her meant she'd thought of the house more fondly than if they'd stayed. If she'd suffered the insecurities of adolescence within those walls, revised for exams, cried over terrible boyfriends, returned frustrated and tired from her first jobs, would she have continued to love the place? Maybe the perfect home existed only in her apple blossom-tinted memory?

"There's no rush," she told Leo. "There's space in our bedroom for a cot. That's all she'll need for a while."

"She?"

"Yes, I think so."

Boy or girl, the child would grow and want room to play, for privacy, and would benefit from a permanent home. The flat wasn't big enough for that, not if they had the choice to move somewhere bigger – which they did. Relocating before the birth seemed sensible. Despite all that, Mandy was again reluctant to move.

They had many happy memories in their flat. The laughter as they and friends painstakingly removed every stubborn scrap of woodchip, only to discover the state of the walls underneath meant they had to replace it with something similar, still seemed to echo faintly. They'd had the daftest dinner parties with their guests eating takeaway meals on the sofa while Mandy and Leo tried to share the footstool without spilling chow mein on the carpet.

In that flat they'd spent a little time arguing and a lot making up. They'd rested there after working so hard on their business and celebrated as it succeeded and they were able to pay off the loans which got them started. Their child had been conceived there. The seven years they'd lived in the flat were the longest period she'd stayed in one place, so the flat was the closest she'd had to a permanent home. But moving on was the right thing to do and Mandy would be happy – she always was in the end.

"Come on then, let's start looking," she said.

Leo surprised her by telling the estate agent they'd prefer a garden with a large apple tree in it. She'd asked him about that later.

"I promised your dad that as soon as I could, I'd have you living somewhere with one."

"You were trying to keep to that whenever you suggested moving before?"

He nodded.

"I'm sorry, love. I didn't understand."

"Neither did I. It's taken time to see what you really need. If we'd moved as soon as we could afford any house with enough garden for an apple tree, I'd probably have been looking to move again by now. You don't want disruption and gradual steps up the property ladder, you want a permanent home."

Once she saw Leo really did understand Mandy put more enthusiasm into house hunting, but her due date was approaching fast and it was increasingly unlikely they'd complete a purchase before the baby was born.

"I'm sorry, love, but can we stop looking?" Mandy asked. "I feel as though we're going to be pushed into a hasty decision."

"I know what you mean. That lovely thatched place, with nowhere to park – I told myself it didn't matter as we could leave the car at work and walk home, but that won't work when we have the baby. I don't want to make a choice we regret."

Their daughter was born right on schedule after an exhausting, but uncomplicated labour. As Mandy had said, there was just room in the flat for a cot, but she'd not appreciated how much other stuff was required. One of those things was a child development book, which informed them young Sally would most likely be crawling and chewing everything in sight from six to ten months of age.

When Mandy looked at the flat's tiny floor area, with all the nooks and crannies which were so difficult to keep clean, and the pretty Victorian fire grates she suspected had been blacked with lead, it was her turn to say they really must move.

With their precise requirements, and the fact they were only prepared to look at houses within a small area, it wasn't often that suitable properties became available. When they did, the little family viewed them together. That made it easier to judge if it was a good place to raise a child. When Sally was six months old, although thankfully still not crawling, they looked at somewhere which had been empty for a long time, but only recently put up for sale.

At first sight it wasn't promising, but they'd learned to look beyond the superficial. Underneath the heavy evergreen shrubs stopping light flood in through the big windows, the grubby paintwork, peeling paper and dusty floors it was a good sized home, conveniently laid out, surrounded by garden and a very short walk from their business premises. As they walked round Sally gurgled with delight.

"I think this is it," Mandy said.

"I think so too."

They went back several times to look round, to be sure. Each time they made plans – which room would be theirs and which the nursery, whether they wanted an ensuite for themselves, or one huge family bathroom and what colour to paint the walls.

"This could be a utility room, with our own washing machine and somewhere to put coats and boots, so we don't bring in mud from the garden," Leo suggested. "There would be space for a deep freeze too."

"And we'll have an actual dining room. And a proper kitchen. We'll be able to have dinner parties where I actually cook, not ring for a Chinese."

"There's posh! Next you'll be wanting enough chairs so everyone can sit at the same time."

"I certainly will! First though, we'd better put in an offer."

"You're sure?"

"Positive."

To Mandy and Leo, whose child was becoming increasingly mobile and inquisitive, the process seemed very slow, but at last they were given a date to move. Everything then seemed a mad rush. They had furniture to order, plumbing and wiring to be sorted, everything to scrub and Sally's room to decorate.

On their first night the house was far from perfect, but they saw nothing but the potential of the place.

"We're all going to be very happy here," Mandy said after Leo had put Sally to bed.

"We are. I'm just sorry there's no apple tree – yet."

"I've been thinking about that. Planting a sapling, watching it getting bigger every day and knowing that one day our children will play in it, will make this house a home more than having a big tree here already would have done."

"I'm glad you said that… and did you say children?"

"Hmmm. I wasn't sure at first whether it was just the excitement of the move, but I've just done a test. It seemed right to do it here – and I'm pregnant again."

"That's wonderful!" He hugged and kissed her. "Actually I have a surprise for you. It's not as good as another baby of course, but I hope you'll like it."

He led her out into the garden and showed her two small pots with twigs in.

"Apple trees?" though she didn't need to ask. What else would her darling husband have bought for their first, and last, home. "But why two? Had you guessed?" she gestured to her belly.

"No. Although I did hope we'd have another child. I got two because I thought that as well as a swing we could have a hammock. It'll take a long time until the trees are big enough, but I didn't think you'd mind waiting."

"I'm not waiting any more. At last I'm home."

6. The Memory Garden

"Sorry, what did you say?" Rhonda asked her daughter.

"Everything's loaded up ready to go. Would you like to stop for lunch now, or get straight off?"

"I'm not quite ready to go."

"Oh, Mum." Marion hugged her. "I know it's hard, but it is for the best."

"Of course it is." Rhonda was agreeing with both statements. The decision to sell the house she'd lived in since her wedding day fifty-five years ago had been difficult one, but it had also been the right one. The old house needed work; noisy, disruptive work. It was too big for her on her own and took too much of her energy to keep it looking nice. Energy she'd far rather use for other things, such as playing with the great-grandchildren, days out, having a go at yoga. The place she was going to was lovely and she had friends already living there. She'd be looked after as much as she needed, but not more than she wanted. Rhonda was sure she'd be very happy once she settled in.

"Why don't you all go off and buy us some nice food and we'll have one last picnic in the garden before we go?" she suggested. It took her a few moments to list what she'd like to eat, and persuade not just Marion, but the rest of the family to go shopping for it. Rhonda's lunch request would, she knew, mean they had to go to at least two different places. She was grateful for their help and company, especially today, but wanted just a little time to herself.

Once alone, Rhonda took a last walk round her treasured garden. The autumn leaves looked at their best now and although she loved the carpet of colour they made as they fell, she wasn't sorry she was going before they'd need to be raked up. She allowed her hand to trail through the myrtle bush she'd grown from a piece in her bridal bouquet. Her touch released a eucalyptus like scent. It had taken a battering now and then in cold winters, but had survived everything the British weather could through at it and rewarded her care with fragrant white flowers every summer. Her Frank used to bring her a sprig of it with her morning tea on their anniversaries. These last three years she'd picked it for him and laid it on his grave.

She moved on from the myrtle to the roses Ruby Wedding and Ruby Anniversary she and Frank had been given by their children after forty years of marriage. These were separated by a ruby red camellia bush, a gift from Frank at the same time. In the same bed she had a selection of golden flowered or foliage plants they'd received a decade later. Brilliant orange calendula further brightened the collection. They still self seeded around from the plants originally grown by her children.

Rhonda had other plants which she'd been given as gifts, sometimes bought from gardens on days out, sometimes dug from a friend's garden. She had a scrapbook showing the plant in its glory, next to a photo of whoever had given it to her. Sometimes she forgot the proper name of a plant, but still recalled how she'd come to own it.

Holidays also often resulted in something new for the garden. If they didn't come back with a plant they'd have bulbs or seeds, or perhaps just a photograph of a planting combination she'd like to try. A few times they'd snaffled a cutting or seed-head on a day out. These plants too were in her scrapbook, along with a shot of the appropriate location.

There were so many memories all around her. The strawberry bed which had been a favourite spot of the children and then grandchildren. A hydrangea was blooming well despite being almost destroyed after an over enthusiastic water fight one hot day many years ago. Wildflowers grew in a spot opened up after a gale tore down the ancient apple tree which had provided fruit for countless pies. She remembered how devastated she'd felt when she'd seen the wreckage, but the tree was soon cleared away. Its wood was used for warm fires and insect habitats and the area seeded over with a wildflower mix. Now it was alive with the hum of bees and flutter of butterflies.

Rhonda went inside to wash her hands ready for the lunch which would arrive any minute. The house she didn't mind leaving, not really. She'd been happy there, but it was draughty and difficult to clean. The stairs were steep and uneven, the plumbing a touch temperamental. She was taking some of her favourite furniture, so would still be able to sit in her comfy chair to read from books stored in the bookcase she and Frank bought just after moving in. The new people had bought some items from her, which she was pleased about. The old dresser had been built to fit the kitchen and would look odd anywhere else. She knew they already loved the house and were likely to look after it. The garden though… so many people didn't have any interest in gardening. No reason why they should of course. Each to his own and all that, but the thought of her borders being covered in gravel for a parking space and the fruit beds grassed over for a football pitch!

Still it was a family moving in. The children would play outside sometimes and maybe there would be barbecues. They'd enjoy it in their own way. Many of the plants she'd see again as her family had taken cuttings, seeds and divisions over the years and so filled their own gardens with the plants Rhonda loved. She'd have to be content with that and her memories and the photos.

Oh yes, the photos. She placed an envelope on the kitchen table, which was also staying right where it belonged. She'd selected twelve photographs showing the garden in each month of the year. Maybe those would encourage the new people not to make hasty decisions. Rhonda left a few other things too. The lady had expressed delight in all her copper pots and pans hanging in the kitchen. Rhonda's daughter-in-law, the only serious cook in the family, took a few.

"I'd love to take more, but I don't have the room and wouldn't use them all in any case. Perhaps you can sell them. It would be such a shame if they weren't used."

When the contents of the house were sold, the only interest shown in the pots was to use them as ornaments in a fancy restaurant. Rhonda had refused the offer and left them in place and a note saying they were her gift to the new owners if they'd like them, but if not could they please donate them to a charity.

"Mum?" Marion called as she walked up the path.

"Just coming." Rhonda stepped out to greet her, without even glancing out the window for a final look at the garden. "I've changed my mind. Let's go straight to the new place and have the picnic there. There are plenty of chairs and benches in the garden and you marked which box holds the kettle and all that so we can have a cup of tea if we like."

Rhonda took time unpacking and settling into her new home. Not because she was unhappy with her comfortable flat and the communal areas, but because she was so busy. Her new neighbours often went together on coach trips to gardens or stately homes. They went out for meals and walks and belonged to clubs. They held tea parties and sing-songs, enjoyed crafts and had a reading group and yoga lessons. Rhonda was hardly left time to water the plants she'd brought with her and which now resided in pots outside her window.

Not long after she moved, Rhonda received a letter from the family who now lived in her old home. They enclosed her photos, thanking her for the chance to see them and saying they'd taken copies for future reference. They added a few more, showing themselves in the garden and plants they'd brought with them from their previous home. Rhonda noticed several pots of twiggy specimens she suspected were small acers and wondered where they'd plant them. They'd look lovely in front of the holly bush, if they cut it back to make a more room and let the sun backlight the gorgeously coloured leaves.

They thanked her for the pots. 'Thank you so much! I love cooking so they'll be well used. I plan to make strawberry jam if children don't eat all the fruit.'

Rhonda smiled. It would take a lot of very hungry children to eat all the fruit that patch yielded, so she was confident that come summer her old home would once again be filled with the scent of jam bubbling away in the huge preserving pan.

When Marion visited, Rhonda showed her the letter.

"They've invited you to go and look at the garden anytime. Would you like me to take you?"

"No. They'll have made changes already, I expect, and it'd upset me to see. Let me keep my memories."

The next time Rhonda had a quiet afternoon she made herself a pot of tea and got out her scrapbook. There was picture of Marion holding the hosta she'd given her one Easter. It was gorgeous then, Rhonda remembered, but hadn't stayed that way. It had been a martyr to slugs, even though she put down crushed eggshells to deter them. The leaves never lasted more than a week in full glory before they were full of holes.

Another photo showed Frank fixing up an archway for honeysuckle and jasmine. He'd made a really good job of it. When the plants had bloomed it had smelled wonderful, and looked so romantic, but it wasn't always pleasant to walk underneath. After rain, or even heavy dew, it dripped. The jasmine grew so vigorously a person had to fight their way through foliage by summer's end.

Some photos showed plants which had later been consumed by caterpillars or got swamped by vigorous neighbours. None of the photos showed the amount of work needed to keep it looking good. They didn't show any untidy areas, or reproach her for her mistakes.

There was a tap at her door.

"Come in," she called to her friend Anthea.

"We've just found out there's a flower show on in the next village tomorrow. Seemed a funny time to have it, but apparently a lot of local gardeners are very keen on hellebores, daphnes and winter blooming heathers. There's room for you in the taxi if you'd like to come?"

"Let me put the kettle on and you can tell me all about it." As Rhonda set out mugs, she recalled visiting the more usual summer versions of such shows when she first grew interested in gardening. Back then they'd frustrated her as her own blooms and produce never reached such a high standard as those displaying cards printed in red with 'First' on them.

"It's not real gardening, love," Frank had said.

She'd known he was right and that to show one vase of perfect blooms the grower had to cultivate rows of plants, protect them and nurture them. Still, she'd decided to stop going. That had been many years ago.

Now she wouldn't have to mentally compare the flawless exhibits with her own efforts. Instead she could compare them to the garden shown in her scrapbook. In it every plant was always in bloom or fruit and there was never a slug or greenfly in sight. Every photograph showed pots and borders, blooms and leaves at their very best, which is exactly how Rhonda chose to remember her beloved garden.

Rhonda's friend told her where the flower show was to be held. "They're doing cream teas and at the end they're selling the exhibits to raise money for charity. Do say you'll come."

"I'd like that very much, thank you." She'd buy herself some real perfect flowers, to add to the many hundreds which bloomed in her memory garden.

7. Nurturing Nature

"I was thinking," Joe said. "We could have lunch at The Slipped Knot on Sunday."

Marcia was tempted to say yes immediately. The pub did a lovely carvery roast and the most amazing lemon meringue sundae. It was also near a garden nursery which specialised in wild flowers. She wanted to create a tiny patch of nature in a big pot outside her front door. Much as she'd love one, she didn't have space to plant anything resembling a proper meadow. There was plenty of room in Joe's garden but if she did anything there which seemed she was making herself at home, he'd ask her to marry him again. It wasn't fair to encourage and then disappoint him.

A potful of plants wouldn't be as directly beneficial to wildlife as converting Joe's lawn, but might do as much good in the long run. Several of her neighbours' children took an interest in what she grew. They enjoyed making snapdragons open their petal mouths, and liked sniffing the mint, lemon verbena and basil leaves. They were even more keen to sample the fragrant strawberries, tangy tomatoes and spicy radishes. Sometimes they helped Marcia with planting and watering.

If she grew wildflowers with them, attracted a few flying creatures and creepy crawlies, perhaps they'd learn to value nature. Lots of children did like such things, Marcia knew, and she loved encouraging them… Most of them, anyway. Sometimes getting involved was just too awkward. That's why she didn't immediately say yes to lunch.

"Sunday?" she queried. "I thought it was your weekend to have Aiden?"

"It is. We'd have plenty of time for lunch and then bowling or something like that before taking him back."

"Sorry, I've… um… got things to do."

"What is it with you and Aiden? I was sure the two of you had hit it off. He really likes you."

"It's not that I don't like him." That was true. He was a sweet and intelligent nine-year-old. She'd been delighted when he wrote about their bug hunt for a school assignment. He'd illustrated it with correctly identified (although creatively spelled) caterpillars and beetles. Another time he drew a flattering sketch of Marcia – her smile had been wider than her hips!

"What is it then? Lately you avoid him whenever you can."

It wasn't Aiden himself who was the problem, but the fact Joe stayed for a cup of tea when he picked the boy up or read him a bedtime story after taking him home, even when Marcia was waiting in the car. Heaven knows how long he stayed when she wasn't.

Marcia never went in. Seeing Aiden's parents with their son reminded her of the love which created him. How could she explain that troubled her and she felt Joe's previous relationship was part of his past and nothing to do with her? When she'd tried before she knew she seemed jealous – and she wasn't, or at least didn't want to be.

Marcia understood Joe wanted to spend time with his son. That was only natural and she'd think less of him if he didn't. But why did he so often choose to do so in the company of his ex-wife? They went to school plays, birthday parties and sports days together. At one time Marcia hadn't minded as it was a good way to lessen the impact of the divorce on Aiden, but the more she came to love Joe, the more it bothered her. Maybe her jealous streak was wider than she'd realised?

"I just think you should spend time with him on your own," Marcia said. It wasn't quite what she meant, but saying how she felt… That wasn't easy, not if it wasn't exactly what the other person wanted to hear.

"I can spend the whole day with Aiden on Saturday. You're out then anyway, aren't you?"

He sounded annoyed. Was that because she was avoiding Aiden, or because she'd been evasive about her plans for the weekend? Perhaps ironically, she was meeting her ex-husband. She didn't know how Joe would feel about that and probably nothing would come of it, so why risk causing upset by mentioning the fact?

The call had been something of a shock – she hadn't exchanged a word with Bryan since the divorce was finalised three years previously and hadn't expected him to have kept hold of her mobile number. The split, which Marcia knew she'd made worse than it needed to be, had been a big upheaval for them both. They'd been business partners as well as husband and wife.

Bryan hadn't wasted much time on small talk before getting to the point. "It's about Little Mallow Copse. The place has changed hands and the new owners have offered me the contract to maintain it. They said they'd like the original team if possible, so I was wondering if you fancied working with me again?"

Marcia wasn't sure that was a good idea, but wanted to see the garden they'd created as a habitat for wildlife. By now it would be mature enough to do the job it was meant for. Visiting with him was her only opportunity to do so as it was in the grounds of an exclusive and discreet hotel. The general public couldn't just wander in for a look round.

"I'm not sure I'll have time," she said in answer to Bryan's suggestion.

"I know you, Marcia. You're just saying that to avoid what you think might be a difficult situation. It'll only be a couple of days a month and you've just told me you work freelance, so you'd manage it if you wanted to."

He was right on both counts.

"Come with me on Saturday and we'll see what needs doing, and work out hours and terms if you decide you can stand working with me."

"Oh, all right, but I'm not promising anything and just to be clear, there's no chance of us getting back together."

"My fiancée will be pleased to hear that."

"Oh. How long have you known her?"

"A couple of years."

The same as her and Joe then.

Bryan arranged when and where to pick her up, then ended the call.

Meeting her ex again was just as awkward as he'd suggested and she'd feared. First she stumbled over congratulating him on his engagement, something she should have done on the telephone, but hadn't quite been able to manage. She was pleased he didn't seem to expect, and she didn't feel, jealousy.

"Thanks, I hope you find someone who'll make you happy too."

She hadn't known what to say – just as she hadn't whenever Joe proposed to her. They discussed the weather during the drive to the hotel.

"How is the copse looking now?" Marcia asked, immediately realising that was a daft thing to say moments before she'd see for herself.

"I don't know. I thought we should both see it together."

Marcia was saved from having to respond to that by the fact they'd arrived, and Bryan was giving their details to someone via a microphone set into the high brick wall. Solid wooden gates swung open to admit them and Bryan drove round to the staff carpark at the back of the hotel. So far everything looked pretty much as she recalled it, but that wasn't true of the copse.

Saplings which were little more than leafy twigs when they'd planted them were now well on the way to being a wood. The pond which had been an almost bare stretch of water was now thickly margined with colourful iris, water mint, brooklime and purple loosestrife. Dragonflies skimmed across the surface and birds drank from the shallows.

And the meadow! When she'd last seen it the wildflowers were just beginning to establish, but only the different shapes of their leaves hinted at the floral display to come. Now it was studded with brilliant white ox eye daisies, pink campions, several varieties of scabious in shades of blue and mauve, gleaming buttercups, robust knapweed, delicate lady's bedstraw… It was glorious and buzzed with life. Bees, lacewings and butterflies danced from blossom to blossom.

As they walked round, inspecting it more closely, Marcia saw the pond's reflective qualities were lost to a layer of duckweed, a big patch of invasive hogweed had become established in the meadow, some trees were smothered in ivy. If Little Mallow Copse was left to itself, the strongest plants would swamp and kill the rest – a natural process perhaps, but not a pretty one. Many things were in need of attention to keep it packed with so many different species of plants and wildlife, and provide the picturesque garden the hotel required. Even so…

"It's wonderful. Just as good as we'd hoped," she said.

"It is. You made great plant choices."

"And you designed it well."

As they grinned at each other it occurred to Marcia that maybe after everything they quite liked each other. Her previous strong feelings for him had gone – both the love she'd once felt and the terrible sadness at the time of their split. He too must have forgiven, or forgotten, or at least decided to move on.

"We were a good team when it came to this sort of thing," Bryan said. "Do you think we could be again?"

She thought maybe they could. They'd been so young when they married and had both changed a lot, grown up and grown apart. If they worked together now, they'd have to build a new relationship. They'd never be close as they once were, but there were still things they shared, which they both cared about. They could be colleagues and maybe eventually become friends.

"All right, but the pay better be good!"

They agreed terms for the work she'd do, and arranged when they'd make a start. As Bryan drove her home he said, "My fiancée might like to come with us sometimes. She's a pretty good artist and the copse would make a great subject."

"What a lovely idea," Marcia said. She had no reason to dislike the new woman in Bryan's life and hoped to prove that went both ways.

As soon as she got in, Marcia switched on the kettle to make a much-needed cup of tea. She was still half surprised by the whole thing, but felt confident she'd been right to agree. By co-operating, they could nurture that wonderful garden and watch it grow. As Bryan said, they'd made a good team in that way. The fact they were no longer together in a romantic sense needn't change that.

Oh! Joe and his ex-wife had created Aiden together. They were no longer a couple, but they still shared the parenting. They both loved the boy and wanted to nurture him and watch him grow. Of course they did. What she'd wished, that Joe's former relationship with his ex was in the past and nothing to do with her, had been true all along.

For once Marcia had been right to keep quiet about how she felt, to avoid the awkwardness of admitting her jealousy of Aiden's mother. That had been a piece of luck, and not proof that keeping quiet, letting things roll on without any input from her, was always the best idea. Generally it wasn't. Her repeated refusals to discuss it when Bryan said their marriage wasn't working had been a mistake. All she'd achieved was to drag out the end until they were both miserable. She couldn't change that now, but there were other mistakes she could be put right.

Marcia rang Joe. "About lunch tomorrow, is it too late to say yes?"

"Not at all. I'll ring The Slipped Knot and ask them to make it a table for three."

"Thanks. Make sure they keep a lemon meringue sundae for me. But before you do, could I have a quick word with Aiden? I want to ask him if instead of going bowling, he'd mind if we went to the garden centre and then got to work on that disgrace you call a lawn. If I'm going to marry you, I'll want a nice wildflower meadow in the garden to encourage lots of wildlife."

"I think he'd love that, and I know I would."

It wouldn't be easy becoming the stepmother of a boy she'd recently been so standoffish with. There would be awkward conversations to come, such as telling her future husband she'd be working with her former one. Even so, she had no hesitation in replying, "Me too, Joe. And Joe, I love you."

8. Thank Goodness For Colin

Cynthia had only just got Colin settled inside her new home before she spotted her first visitor walking up the path.

"It's the neighbour who was so friendly when I viewed the house," she told Colin. "I hope I haven't upset her with my parking." Cynthia's car was outside her neighbour's property, in order to leave room for the furniture delivery van.

She stepped outside. "Hello again. I… "

"Hello! Welcome to Bluebell Crescent! I hope you'll be very happy here."

"Thank you. I'm sure I shall, once I've …"

"You'll need to get settled of course. Anything I can do to help, just ask."

"Actually, is there a takeaway nearby? I won't be ready to cook anything, nor feel like going out tonight." She added that last bit in a rush in case it seemed she was angling for an invitation. She'd hate it herself if a neighbour was too pushy or wanted to be in her pocket all the time.

"There's nowhere very near, but some do deliveries. I'll dig out the leaflets."

She did – and brought a tray of tea and biscuits for Cynthia and the removal men.

"Garibaldis, my favourite!" Cynthia said.

It seemed she'd been extremely fortunate in buying this particular house, especially as it was pure chance she had. On a whim she'd visited the town in which she'd grown up.

The place had changed a great deal, but mostly for the better.

"Or maybe it's me who's changed?" she suggested to Colin. "The library, museum and peaceful garden must have been there when I was a teenager. I didn't appreciate such things then."

Cynthia had glanced in the estate agent's window and spotted what seemed the perfect home from which to enjoy her retirement. The modern terrace would be easy to look after and leave her enough money to travel. She'd been thinking of an apartment, so as not to have a garden to worry about when she was away, but the backyard had just a few pretty little trees growing through gravel.

"A bit of raking every autumn seems a fair exchange for a pleasant outside space to sit with a drink," she told Colin.

She'd been putting the last of the packing materials out in the bin a few days later when her neighbour called round to provide an overwhelming amount of information about busses, shops, and local organisations. "I'm Judy by the way. Judy Calf and my husband is Derek. Not that you'll see much of him! Always down the bar he is, or playing golf."

"I'm Cynthia Martin."

"No!" Judy squinted at Cynthia. "You can't be! My best friend at school was Cynthia Martin. I was Judy Mason back then, so we were next to each other in the register – and everywhere else!"

Cynthia would never have recognised Judy, whom she'd not spoken to for fifty years, from her appearance, but that description brought it all back. "And we're next to each other once again."

"It is then? It really is you?"

Cynthia admitted being herself.

"You simply must come to dinner tonight," Judy said.

It was a common phrase, but Cynthia felt she really wasn't being given much choice in the matter. "Oh no, I couldn't…"

"Nonsense. It'll be nice to have someone who appreciates me cooking for them. Derek takes getting a hot meal for granted."

"Oh…"

"And while you're there you can look at how we've decorated the place. It might give you some ideas for yours. Of course, not having a husband you'll need to get a man in to do it."

"Well, I…"

"Better really. Takes Derek ages to get around to doing it, and the mess he makes! Anyway, see you at seven."

"Oh dear, Colin. I think I might be needing your help!" Cynthia said as soon as she got back inside. She made tea for herself and gave Colin water. "It's exaggerating to say Judy and I were best friends. She didn't have any others and I was too shy to ask her to give me some space."

Judy showed Cynthia round her house. Although very full, it was extremely clean and tidy. Every window had spotless lace curtains. Every sill held flowering plants so immaculate Judy wanted to touch one to check they were real. The well equipped kitchen was modern, the three piece suite looked new. There was nothing Cynthia could have found fault with, had she wished to try, but there was nothing in it to inspire her either. Fortunately Judy had no interest in Cynthia's opinions, she just wanted to show off her top-of-the-range appliances, luxurious carpeting throughout and triple-glazed windows.

"Of course mine being semi-detached, and considerably larger than yours, you won't be able to make it look quite the same."

Cynthia didn't mention Judy's home was technically an end terrace and she had no wish to copy her boring decor. That would have been rude and in any case, she hardly got a word in.

Cynthia didn't see Derek until she was ushered into the dining room.

"You sit yourself down and I'll bring dinner through," Judy instructed.

"Can I do anything to help?" Cynthia asked.

"No, I know where everything is and I'll just get in a muddle if I don't do it all myself."

The meal was ridiculously elaborate for a midweek supper with a neighbour and meant Judy was constantly leaving the room to fetch something. That allowed Cynthia to chat with Derek who seemed very pleasant.

When Judy was in the room she explained the complicated procedures she'd gone through to create the meal. It all tasted quite nice, but probably would have done had Judy simply chopped and steamed a selection of vegetables, not turned potatoes, Julienned carrots, fried sprouts in truffle scented oil and individually skinned the broad beans.

Cynthia hardly got to speak until Judy asked how she'd like her coffee.

"I won't, thanks. Better get back to Colin." She used the rare moment of silence that produced to say goodbye to Derek and make her escape.

Over the next few weeks Cynthia used a version of that excuse to avoid getting involved in Judy's life. She had explanations ready for why Judy never saw Colin – his lack of mobility and quiet, prickly personality – but they were rarely needed. Prying into other people's lives wasn't one of Judy's faults.

Judy was in some ways an excellent neighbour. Always willing to take in parcels, hold spare keys and let in tradespeople. She fetched shopping and cooked meals for residents of Bluebell Crescent who were unable to do so themselves, and visited them in hospital should they be admitted. No one had to explain why such help was required, or even ask for it, they simply had to listen to Judy saying how ungrateful some people were for all she tried to do for them.

Cynthia was informed that Derek, who was always under Judy's feet or making a mess, ignored her half the time and was out the rest. Judy also revealed why she was an expert on all the local organisations – she was either the chairperson or on the committee of most of them.

"They're lucky to have you," Cynthia said and meant it. Judy would be good at getting things done, or doing them herself if no one matched her exacting standards. She tried to involve Cynthia in a variety of roles.

"Sorry, it's Colin you see. I don't like to commit myself to anything."

The last part was completely true, but Colin was more the result than the cause of that. For a long time Cynthia had been looking forward to the freedom of retirement. No need to fit her holiday around meetings, deadlines and colleagues. No rows of houseplants needing constant care. No husband to complain about constantly. No clubs and groups unable to manage without her. Thanks to Colin, Cynthia never felt alone, but could come and go just as she liked, whether it was a stroll down the library or a three week safari.

"Colin likes the sun," Cynthia said to explain that. The statement was after all perfectly true and she was prevented from saying more by Judy moaning Derek never took her away.

"You be careful," Judy cautioned. "Tourist places are full of foreigners and the food will be strange."

"I'll watch out for that." Meeting interesting new people was among her reasons for wishing to travel.

Just before she left for her trip, Cynthia gave one last drink of water to her leaving present from work. It was a shame she couldn't take Colin the cactus with her, but he'd be just fine enjoying the sunshine on the kitchen windowsill until she returned.

9. Positively Negative

It was a lovely day and Eve was setting off to meet her friend Alice for lunch and a good laugh. She'd left a nice chicken salad for her husband George, who'd assured her he was looking forward to sitting in the garden with a book after he'd cut the grass.

Eve stepped out her front door at exactly the same time as her neighbour was locking hers. "Good morning, Laura," she called. Eve noticed the strained look on the other woman's face and felt her own smile slip in sympathy.

Before Eve could ask what was wrong, Laura put up a hand in a firm 'stop' gesture. "Whatever it is, don't say it. I just can't deal with your constant negativity today!"

Eve was so shocked she stood speechless as Laura marched down her path, got in her car and drove away. This was so unlike Laura. She might not always have time for a chat, but she was never so abrupt and never even hinted that a conversation with Eve would be anything but a pleasure.

Twenty-five years they'd been neighbours. They took in parcels for each other, watered the garden during holidays, held each other's door keys in case of emergencies. Laura's children's Christmas presents were hidden in Eve's home.

They'd never fallen out. There had been times that could have happened. When Laura's children were small they were sometimes a bit of a nuisance, always losing toys into Eve's garden, then climbing the fence to retrieve them and causing damage in the process.

Eve had remembered when her own children were small and mischievous. Not bad, just high spirited and oblivious to anyone but themselves. She'd had a word with Laura and they'd come up with a plan. The children were to knock on the front door and ask for their toys back, not more than once a day. Laura had thanked Eve for her patience and said the arrangement was teaching the children to be more careful.

More recently they'd held different opinions on political matters, but had agreed to disagree. Laura wasn't ever confrontational. She'd give you an honest opinion if you asked for it, but otherwise seemed to live by the maxim that if you couldn't think of anything good to say then say nothing.

So what had prompted today's outburst?

A horrible thought struck Eve. Maybe Laura had said it because she thought it was true. That it was such a severe issue she simply couldn't keep quiet.

'Constant negativity' she'd said. Eve thought back to their last few conversations. Eve had seen Laura hanging out the washing and warned her rain was forecast, mentioned roadworks she and George were held up by and advised her to allow extra time if she was driving that way, and explained she'd let herself in to close a window Laura had left open as it might have been an invitation to thieves. Eve had been trying to help, but yes those remarks could all be seen as negative.

Eve didn't think she was particularly negative. She was realistic and liked to plan for all eventualities, which meant she considered what could go wrong, but only to stop such things happening or minimise them if they did. If a grandchild grazed their knee Eve always had a soothing antiseptic wipe, and plaster, if needed. That wasn't because she wanted them to fall, just that she knew from experience it was likely to happen. The sooner it was cleaned and kissed better the sooner the child would be off playing again. It wasn't as though she tried to stop them having fun in case something went wrong.

But she was carrying an umbrella on a beautiful spring day 'just in case', she had aspirin in her bag, and a mini sewing kit in case of lost buttons or unstitched hems and all sorts of other bits and pieces to deal with problems which she must subconsciously expect to arise.

Laura let herself back into the house.

"What's wrong?" George asked.

"Oh dear. It's true then."

"What is?

"That I'm always negative. I must be if the first thing you think when you see me is that I have a problem to report."

"I only thought that because you were off to see Alice and you've come back after a few minutes looking really unhappy. What's happened, love?"

She told him about Laura's outburst.

"That's very unlike her. She must be having a bad day."

Being in a bad mood would explain Laura being so abrupt, but didn't fully account for the words she'd used. "You don't think it's true?" Eve asked.

"Would you have married me if it was?"

That was a good point. There had been plenty of people who'd said it wouldn't work. They were too young. Too different. He'd gone to the grammar school and was at university studying engineering. She'd barely scraped her 11 plus and her shop job would have to support them both until he qualified. Her family went to church, his didn't. Eve had said none of that mattered as they loved each other, and she'd been proved right. But that was over fifty years ago.

"Remember our golden wedding party?" Eve said. "You were positive that having it in the garden, so we could invite more people, would be OK, because you remembered most of our anniversaries were as sunny as the wedding day itself. I remembered the few times it rained and insisted on borrowing a gazebo."

"You were right, love," George said. "If it had rained we couldn't have got everyone in the house."

"But it was blazing hot."

"Which meant the shade of the gazebo was very welcome."

Eve smiled. "Yes, it worked out well in the end."

"Most things you're involved in do, because you're prepared for things to go wrong and are able either to stop them, or at least make them less bad."

"I've been telling myself that, but then I thought about my handbag."

"Let's have a look."

George's opinion of her antiseptic wipes and plasters was the same as Eve's – practical, not pessimistic. The same applied to her sewing kit.

"What about these?" She indicated paper tissues.

"The last time I remember you using those it was to mop up tears of laughter."

"That's right! Alice and I were laughing about… actually I don't recall what set us off, but once we started we couldn't stop."

"It was when a gust of wind caught your skirt and the pair of you started attempting Marilyn impressions."

"Oh, yes we did… But that was a while back. I was thinking of last week." Someone who regularly got into fits of giggles with their friend couldn't be entirely negative, could they? "Thanks George, you've made me feel more positive!" She kissed him goodbye and set off to see Alice, determined to remain positive.

Her bus had already gone, so she had a short wait for another, which was good as it allowed her to chat with the young mother who arrived just after her.

"I'm glad to see someone else here," the woman said over the child's wails. "I don't usually get the bus and don't know when they run."

Eve was able to provide her with a copy of the timetable and restore the child to happy gurgles by sewing the pom-pom back onto her hat.

"You've saved my life!" the young mother said. Clearly that was a massive overstatement, but it left Eve in no doubt she'd made a positive difference.

Just after Eve stepped off the bus she spotted a young couple holding hands on a bench. It was Tish, a colleague of Alice's, and a young man Eve had spotted hanging around the charity shop where they both volunteered. He'd seemed very ill at ease and didn't meet Eve's eyes as she'd said 'excuse me' and walked past him, just to let him know he'd been seen. She'd warned Alice about the possibility he was a shoplifter.

"I don't think that's it. He only comes in when Tish is working. I'm pretty sure it's her and not the merchandise he's interested in," Alice had said.

It seemed Alice had been right. Eve was glad. She watched them for a little while. They looked so happy. Of course they were young and the path of true love didn't always run smooth, but it might work out for them as it had with her and George. And Alice and her Jim come to that. And even if it didn't, happy for a little while was better than never having loved at all… she'd got the quote wrong, but was sure she had the meaning right.

She mentioned seeing the couple when she met Alice – still on time despite going back home for reassurance, as she'd allowed for the possibility of getting held up, just as she always did.

"I'm impressed he got up the nerve to ask her," Eve said. "Tish is delightful, but she's so confident I can imagine that being a problem for some young men. Suppose my negativity had kept them apart? If you'd believed my idea about him being a shoplifter and warned her she might have refused him when he asked her out. Thank you for not passing on my negativity."

"Actually I did tell her and that's what got them together," Alice said. "Turns out she'd noticed him and tried to encourage him, but he'd still not plucked up courage to speak. When I told her what you'd suspected she marched over to him and said, 'There are two theories about you. Either you want to ask me out and are too shy, or you're a shoplifter. What's it going to be – will you buy me a coffee in my next break, or shall I call the police?'" Eve chuckled. "Oh dear, poor boy! It's a wonder he didn't run away."

Over a delicious lunch, Alice assured Eve she wasn't a negative person, just practical. After that they went to a local public garden – not to admire the flower filled beds and borders, but to have a go on the pedalos which had recently been introduced to the formal pond. Eve's tissue supply was once again depleted as they mopped up tears of laughter.

As she rode the bus home, Eve's thoughts drifted back to Laura. It now seemed clear that George was right and their neighbour had been having a bad day. Although we shouldn't do it, under such circumstances it's natural to snap at the first person we encounter. Eve could easily forgive the woman for being human. Hopefully whatever was wrong would now be resolved and they could return to being on friendly terms as though the incident had never happened.

Eve hadn't finished telling George what she and Alice had been up to when there was a knock on the door. She opened up to see Laura on her doorstep

"I'm sorry for snapping at you earlier, will you accept these by way of apology?" She offered a bunch of tulip buds. "Oh dear, I've been carrying them around so long they've wilted. Poor things will never open now." Laura looked close to tears.

"Of course they will. George will put them in water and they'll be fine. Now sit down and tell me what's wrong."

After a few moments thought, Laura did. "It wasn't your negativity I was worried about, but my own. You see my daughter is seeing this man and she's bringing him round this evening. I'm sure it's to say they're getting married."

"That's good, isn't it? Oh! You don't like him?"

"To be honest, I don't really know him. He's very different – he was born abroad, grew up in a very different culture and has a strong accent and… I didn't give him a chance, just thought of all the things which could go wrong and warned her and…"

"I see."

"Do you?" Laura asked.

"It sounds very like when George and I got engaged. Our parents only saw our differences and thought it wouldn't work. They tried to keep us apart, not because of disapproval or unkindness, but because they thought they could save us from getting hurt."

"That is why I'm worried, really it is. But I didn't explain myself at all well, and I confess I was so blinded by my concerns I didn't even try to look for his good points."

"He must have them if your daughter loves him."

"True. I'll make a point of looking for them. How about your parents? Did they come round after you married?"

"They saw sense long before that. Once they expressed their concerns we were able to reassure them we'd thought of all that and were confident we could overcome the difficulties – especially if we had help."

"That's where I've gone wrong. I tried to shut out all the negative thoughts, which involved ignoring their relationship. If I tell her what I'm worried about and offer my support in overcoming those issues, do you think that will put things right?"

Eve grinned. "Yes, I'm positive it will."

10. That's Not Cricket

Beth fiddled with the nozzle on the hosepipe, but nothing happened. Great, just great. This was absolutely the last thing she needed. She thought she'd nearly finished but there were still the pots to do and she knew they'd dry out quickly if not given a good soaking. Now she'd have to use the watering can and it'd take ages and Simon would be fed up – again. For a teenager he'd not had many moody strops, but she didn't doubt one would be on the way if she were late taking him to watch the cricket practice.

Why he wanted to go she couldn't fathom, neither he nor his friends played and he never watched it on television. His taking an interest in something was the most positive move from him for weeks though, so Beth was doing all she could to encourage it.

Muttering slightly under her breath, Beth filled the can directly from the tap. It wasn't as though she had any more interest in gardening than she'd thought Simon had for cricket. The plot and pots she'd been tending for the last few days belonged to her neighbour. Deirdre always looked after Beth's garden, such as it was, when she and her son were away. Naturally Beth had offered to care for Deirdre's pride and joy in return, although she'd rarely left it for longer than a day since Beth and Simon moved next door ten years ago.

Last week Deirdre had said, "I'm going away for a few days soon and the forecast is for dry weather. I wondered if I could possibly ask you to do a bit of watering?"

Despite realising it would be quite a lot of watering, not to mention topping up the bird baths and feeders, Beth had said, "No problem at all. Are you going somewhere nice?"

"Oh yes, my granddaughter's wedding."

"Lovely!"

Beth sighed. It seemed such a thing wasn't ever likely to happen to her. Simon had started to get interested in girls and some liked him, despite his problems. He'd been in an accident as a baby. The relatively minor injuries had seemed, to her, a small price to pay for his survival, but then she hadn't needed surgery and physiotherapy in order to walk properly and didn't get teased at school because half her hand was missing. He'd coped extremely well.

Beth had always focussed on things he could do, not those he couldn't. By the time he was old enough for a paper round, he could cycle without any problems. The doctors were positive that by the time he reached seventeen, he'd be able to drive a car without needing to have it modified. He had a lovely personality too, everyone liked him for his sense of fun.

Simon had struggled to cope when his dad and Beth split up. He'd become withdrawn and took a lot of convincing that his parents wouldn't stop caring about him just because they'd stopped loving each other. He went to stay with his father and stepmother sometimes but had made it clear he wished to live with Beth. When she'd met David, Simon had, not surprisingly, taken a while to warm to him, but at Christmas he bought David a pair of slippers. Beth did wonder if he might have booby trapped them in some way, but no shocks awaited David as he slid in his feet.

They were just ordinary, fairly cheap ones but David had asked, "What's with the slippers? Simon asks me about ten times an hour if I like them. I'm sure he's up to something."

That's when she'd known David was accepted. Simon always played jokes on those he liked. Even as a small child he'd enjoyed doing it. When he learned to tie his shoe laces he'd crawled under tables in restaurants tying other peoples' shoes together, then holding up his damaged hand in an attempt to prove himself innocent. She'd gently pointed out it wouldn't be so funny if someone fell and hurt themselves and he'd been careful after that. Pranks continued, but they were nothing which might harm anyone, not unless you counted their sense of pride.

Simon continued to regularly ask David if he liked the slippers, varying it occasionally with, "Are they comfortable?"

"Very, thank you," David always assured him even though the continued questioning was irritating. By April the slippers were beginning to fall apart, but Simon still asked now and then. His angelic smile on hearing how well they were liked was more than a little suspicious.

Beth too guessed Simon was up to something; but what? He was certainly biding his time. That too was his way. Once, over a series of weeks, he'd looked up recipes and asked Beth to cook them for him. As they were all interesting, healthy choices she'd obliged, even though they meant buying herbs, spices or other ingredients she didn't often use. It wasn't until she'd searched for vanilla essence one day and found it tucked away between olive oil and elderflower cordial that she realised Simon had rearranged the cupboard so the initial letters on each pack spelled out 'I love you Mum'.

In late spring Deirdre, their garden and bird loving neighbour, had found 'thanx 4 seeds' written in crocus flowers across her tiny wildflower meadow.

"It's a present from the birds," Simon had said, repeating the expression Deirdre used whenever a plant showed up in an unexpected location, but failing to suppress his laughter.

Luckily Deirdre found it amusing. She countered with, "How lovely of them! You know, blue daffodils would look superb with those. I don't want to be cheeky, but maybe if I supply my feathered friends with mealworms too, they'll get me a few next year?"

She'd winked at Beth, confirming her suspicion that Simon would find he'd had a joke played on him were he to try buying daffodil bulbs which would produce blue blooms.

Later that month, Beth had done her usual spring clean which included bleaching the net curtains.

"There, just like new," she said as she hung them.

"We should put bleach on David's slippers," Simon said. "Then they'd be like new too."

"I don't think that would work," she started to say, but he'd grabbed them off David's feet and headed for kitchen. He chucked them in the bucket she used for mopping the floor and poured on bleach.

"No, it'll melt them!" Beth warned, far too late.

"Don't worry, Mum. They'll be good as new." Simon waved her out the kitchen.

Two minutes later he appeared with a pair of slippers which did indeed look brand new.

Beth and David stared at them in confusion. No amount of bleach could have done that and in fact Beth remembered she'd used the last on the nets anyway. Once Simon stopped laughing, he revealed that at Christmas he'd bought two identical pairs of slippers, with this prank in mind. Apparently it had been prompted by his mother's remark about bleach restoring the special Christmas tablecloth to a state of snowy white perfection and the memory of her 'just like new' comments when she bleached tea towels and his school shirts.

David and Beth were suitably amused. Partly because it was quite funny, partly because he had new slippers to replace his tatty ones, but mostly because it showed Simon had accepted David as a new addition to his world.

Beth wasn't quite sure how he felt about the other addition. His stepmother was expecting a baby. Beth herself tried to sound pleased about that, hoping this would make things more comfortable. She found it easier to be happy that although Simon was always very polite to his stepmother he never played his tricks on her.

Simon had his eye on a girl, Beth was fairly sure. The name Kirsty came up in conversation even more often than that of his favourite football team.

"He asked me how I'd got you to go out with me," David reported. "I've done my best to give him what advice I can, but I don't know if it'll help at all."

"Thanks for trying."

A few days later Simon came home, locked himself away in his bedroom and only came out for meals all weekend. Kirsty's name wasn't mentioned but Beth guessed he'd asked her out and she said no. Then Simon announced that he was nearly old enough to apply for the navy. Years before he'd expressed an interest in joining and without trying to be too negative Beth had explained he probably wouldn't be able to. She tried again to say that.

"I know I probably can't, but I might as well find out for sure."

David gave him a lift to the recruiting office which Beth was grateful for. He needed someone with him when he got the bad news and she was sure it would be bad. She blamed herself for not realising he'd still held out hope.

When David brought Simon home he went straight to his room again.

"It was a no, of course," David said. "They were nice about it and explained why and everything."

"How did he take it?"

"Not too bad I don't think. We had a bit of a chat on the way back. Oh and we were right about Kirsty. She said no."

"It wasn't because of his hand and things was it?"

"He's not sure, but he did say if that was the reason then maybe he'd be better off without her."

"He's right. Thanks for talking to him, David."

"No bother. Just wish I could cheer him up."

No one could. After a few days Simon was almost back to normal, but there were no jokes. It seemed like he might have turned some kind of corner though with his sudden interest in the cricket. So far he'd only seemed to want to watch, but she was fairly sure the village team would allow him to play if he wanted to. There were always posters up in the hall asking for players of all abilities.

Beth had promised Simon a lift and now she'd be late or would have to leave the watering and come back. What was she thinking? There was no question, she should leave this, give her son a lift to the cricket ground and come back to water afterwards. Simon had reminded her that Deirdre always watered at this time of day, but it surely couldn't matter if she left it an hour or so.

Beth picked up the exasperating hose, intending just to pull it out the way so nobody would trip on it. The rotten piece of tubing choose just that second to decide to work again and drenched Beth in icy water. Great, just great. This was absolutely the last thing she needed. Now she would have to change and would be late driving Simon to the cricket practice after all.

Then she heard it; the sound of smothered giggling. It was Simon, he must have rigged the hose!

"How long have you been waiting to do that?" she demanded.

"Couple of days. Pretending I was interested in cricket was part of it. I had to work it so I didn't make you late for anything important."

"That's something I suppose. Do you know, I've only had two seconds to think of this."

Beth emptied the watering can over his head. There was hardly anything left in it, but hearing his shriek of laughter was just what she needed.

11. The Idea

The girl will be here in a minute. Now what's her name? Pretty name I remember, a flower maybe? Rose, Lily, Daisy? No; it started with an 'M' same as Millie and it was Millie who told me what it meant. Myrtle! That's it, Myrtle.

Why can't I remember names? I'm OK with everything else. I remember that myrtle is a scented bush and brides sometimes have a sprig in their bouquets for luck. I remember how Millie blushed when she talked about weddings and how that gave me *The Idea*. That was before she went in for her hip op.

Another thing I remember; Myrtle's not a girl she's a highly trained professional. Professional what, I don't recall. Job descriptions are as bad as names. Nurse, I suppose must be part of it. Myrtle takes care of the ulcer on my leg and checks I'm doing OK. Says I need looking after. Before Millie got ill, I was thinking of discussing *The Idea* with Myrtle. She's a sensible gir… highly trained professional and she'll understand things from the woman's point of view.

Here she is.

"Come in, Myrtle. How are you today?"

"I'm fine, Henry. What about you and that leg of yours?"

"Both still here."

"Let's have a look then."

I roll up my trouser leg whilst she washes her hands.

I tell her, "It's looking much better and doesn't hurt at all now. That's thanks to all your highly trained professional care, my dear."

She laughs. "I'm glad someone appreciates me."

"Oh?"

"Sorry, it's nothing."

"You can tell me."

"It's just that some patients seem to ignore my advice about basic cleanliness and then wonder why they end up with infections."

"I can see why that would bother you, but really you can't blame them with the way the hospitals carry on."

"What do you mean?"

"Nurses going to and from work in their uniforms and wards not being cleaned and then everyone gets that MRSA and it eats away at them until they die."

"Henry! Hey come on now – what's brought this on?"

Silly fool that I am, I've got tears streaming down my face.

"It's Millie. She went in for her op and now…"

"I remember you said your girlfriend was having a hip replacement. What's happened?"

"She had the op yesterday and I'm told it went fine, but I can't see her as they have an outbreak of MRSA. Now I might never see her again."

Myrtle, bless her, sees I'm embarrassed about being upset. "I could do with a cup of tea. Would it be OK if I made us both one?"

"Of course it would, my dear. I'd have offered you one, but you've usually got to rush off."

"It's time for my lunch break. I've got sandwiches, I'll eat them here if that's OK?"

"Of course. That'd be grand."

To tell the truth, without Millie to visit, I'm already fed up with my own company. Silly really as I've been on my own since I retired from the army. Never bothered me before but since Millie and I started going on outings and things together, I've found I like a bit of female company.

"Oooh, Henry, what gorgeous flowers! Are they for your girlfriend?" she calls from the kitchen.

"I tried to take them to Millie, if that's what you mean."

Myrtle, the cheeky young professional, always calls Millie my girlfriend. Maybe that's what first put *The Idea* into my head?

"Here's your tea. Now tell me what's going on with you and Millie. The way you were talking last time I came, I thought you'd be engaged by now."

"Well, um er…" I'm proper flustered. Surely her high level of training doesn't include mind reading?

"You said you can't visit her because of the MRSA?"

"That's right. They wouldn't let me in and they wouldn't even let me leave her the flowers."

"That's a shame. Look, I'm going up there this afternoon; I've got samples to drop off. You tell me her full name and which ward she's in and I'll see what I can find out."

"She's on Scarsdale ward and it's Millie Hepworth."

"But you'd like it to be Mrs Mortimer?"

"Well… Oh darn it; yes. But what's the use?"

"Don't put yourself down. You're a lovely man and she seems to enjoy your company. Your leg is healing up nicely and there's nothing else wrong with you."

"I can't propose if they won't let me in. Family only they said." If I'd only put *The Idea* into action months ago then maybe that wouldn't have been a problem. "And she could get this MRSA thing."

"It's possible, Henry but not likely because of the precautions they're taking."

"Like not letting me and my flowers in?"

"Exactly. Shall I take a picture of the flowers and see if they'll let me show her that? I'm sure she'll be happy to know you bought them."

"Good idea. I'll get my camera."

"No need, I can use my phone."

Myrtle takes a picture of the flowers and one of me waving to Millie.

"Shall I give her a message? I have an idea there's something you'd like to ask her?"

I chuckle. "We both have an idea, Myrtle dear, but you just tell her to get well quick and that I'll see her as soon as I possibly can. And you take the flowers for yourself if you'd like them. I'll buy more for Millie as soon as she comes home."

"Oh! Thank you so much, Henry. That's very kind of you."

It's a very small reward for giving me the confidence to put *The Idea* into action.

12. Arranging Daffodils

My sister Freya is obsessed with flower arranging. She's tried dragging me to classes.

"It not my sort of thing," I told her.

"Why not?"

"I'd rather be baking."

"Fair point. I don't want you giving that up."

She's very partial to a slice of my lemon drizzle, is Freya. And my coconut sponge, flapjack, sultana scones…

Her flower arrangements are lovely and it seems a nice hobby, or would be if she wasn't persuaded into competing. That's the difference between us. I stick to what I know I can handle; Freya keeps stepping out of her comfort zone. Well, sometimes she steps and occasionally she takes an almighty leap such as agreeing to compete in a sponsored triathlon, despite her lack of co-ordination and the fact the cycling part was mountain biking on an actual mountain. Freya broke her wrist.

I took round freshly baked almond cookies and a bunch of pink tulips. Freya was suitably grateful when I made tea and put that and the cookies in easy reach.

"Seems you've got me flower arranging after all," I said as I shortened a few stems, put the tulips in a jug and shuffled them about so none of the blooms were hidden behind another.

"You've made a really good job of it," she said. "And you have a great eye for colour. They look perfect in this room."

I can recognise flattery with an ulterior motive when it's heaped on thickly enough. "What do you want? Shopping? A lift somewhere?" I asked.

"Both." She told me about the flower arranging competition that weekend. Apparently it was vital that someone called Celia didn't win. "It took me a while to realise it, but she doesn't play fair."

"And you can beat her with a broken wrist?" I asked.

"I have to try."

She reached for her mug with her good arm and winced in pain. "I cracked a few ribs as well…"

We're not twins, but we are close. My theory is she also banged her head but I was the one suffering the symptoms. That's the only explanation I have for what happened next.

"I'd better do this competition instead of you," I said. "I've picked up a few things watching you, and you keep saying I have some artistic ability."

"You do! That's an excellent plan. Maybe some good will come of this."

"Perhaps I can sabotage this Celia's attempts?"

"You won't. You're far too nice to do anything like that. Celia isn't. What she does isn't technically cheating, but she's underhand."

"I'd better get down the florist's and start practising."

"Help yourself to my equipment," Freya offered.

I took everything I could carry.

Daffodils were the cheapest flowers, so I got loads. It seemed wasteful to buy expensive blooms just for me to mangle them, plus the competition theme was spring.

Back in my flat, I stuck the whole lot in a vase I'd borrowed from Freya. They looked lovely massed together. If someone were doing an arrangement for me, that's what I'd like.

I tried all the techniques Freya told me about. I scrunched the wire netting too tightly and couldn't wriggle the stems through. With the foam, the flowers ended up looking startled. The thing with pins in was no good as daffodil stems are hollow.

When Freya phoned on Saturday, to ask how I was doing, I told her I'd had a lightbulb moment. I really had. You see, I'd read somewhere that the guy who invented the lightbulb tried masses of things which didn't work. He said eliminating them wasn't failure but an important stage. I'd almost eliminated all Freya's props, accessories and techniques so must be very close to the answer!

"It's fine, Sis," I assured her. "Piece of cake."

Mentioning cake was a mistake, because I got an urge to bake white chocolate and caramel brownies. They turned out beautifully… about twenty minutes after the florist closed.

Undaunted, I remembered the corner shop sold daffodils and bought the entire stock. Then I recalled that Freya always used supporting greenery and stuff, not just flowers. Pulling a stroke of genius, I called on the lady who has the garden flat below me.

"Would you swap some of your leafy stuff for a bunch of daffs and piece of cake?"

"You help yourself to whatever you want, love," she said. "The shrubs need trimming anyway."

I cut loads of stuff, including pieces of what she told me was forsythia. It was the exact shade of the daffs. Maybe that would create a harmony or something? I decided against further practice. Spontaneity would be my secret weapon.

I arrived at the hall, with armfuls of hedge trimmings, daffodils and equipment. The place was in chaos. One woman was distraught and apologised profusely because she'd stepped on a piece of forsythia a pretty girl had dropped.

"Don't worry, it's fine," the younger one said in a tight-lipped fashion. She obviously didn't mean it.

My suspicions about her identity were confirmed when the lady opposite me murmured to a friend, "I see Celia's up to her tricks again."

"I have plenty of forsythia," I told Celia, brandishing a big piece. "Do take it." I didn't do it for her, but for the other woman who was so upset at the damage she'd done.

"That's really kind of you," Celia said, sounding genuine.

I put my vase on the table, unwrapped all the daffs and plonked them in. Even with all the stuff I had with me, I reckoned anything else I did would make them look worse, but to quote my sister, I had to try.

Looking round for inspiration, I noticed the woman who'd accidentally trodden on Celia's forsythia was helping people. I heard her say, "You could do with a larger bloom at the base, to add weight and make it more balanced." She approached someone else. "That's so pretty! I hope you don't mind me saying, but I think you would be better off with slightly more delicate foliage. Hang on, I'll see if I have anything." She came back with quite big leaves. "So sorry, this is the best I can do. I'm not sure they'll help."

I had a big bunch of some feathery grassy sort of stuff that had been overhanging my neighbour's path. I took it over and they both said how perfect it was.

As I returned, Celia was looking daggers. Hah! Worried about me helping the opposition, was she? I decided to show her how decent people behave and took all my spare bits and pieces around to the other competitors.

"Please help yourself if any of it will be useful," I offered.

When I went back to my own area, Celia was crying. She was shaking so badly she couldn't get the flower stem into the foam. Freya had said she was awful, and wanted her to be beaten, but I didn't think she'd want to see her quite so miserable.

"Are you OK?" It was a stupid question, but she didn't snap my head off.

"Low blood sugar, I think. I haven't had time to eat."

"You'll make yourself ill. Stop for a minute and get yourself some food."

"I can't, I have so much to do."

She had. Her arrangement was less complete than it had been before I set off to distribute bits of shrub.

"You've taken things out," I said.

"I'm not sure ranunculus really are spring flowers."

I couldn't help; I only knew which were the ranunculus as they were piled in a heap. "Did she say they aren't?" I indicated the helpful woman.

"Yes." That tight-lipped look was back.

"She seems to know what she's talking about."

"Yes."

The poor girl was really in a state. I fetched her some of my chocolate brownies and insisted she eat while I phoned Freya to ask about the ranunculus. My sister definitely wouldn't want Celia beaten because she passed out before finishing her arrangement.

"They're spring flowers," she told me. "But spring is just the theme. Anything which looks the part is OK."

I relayed that information to Celia.

"Was that Freya Clarke?"

"Yes, she's my sister. That's why I'm here making a fool of myself."

Celia perked up after that. It's amazing what chocolate brownies can do. We chatted as she worked.

"Say if I'm putting you off," I said.

"No, it helps. I get so stressed in these competitions."

That's when I sussed Celia wasn't really horrible, just acted so under pressure.

"I probably would too, if I hadn't given up," I admitted. Until then I'd been standing so she couldn't see my plonked 'arrangement' of daffodils.

"You've still got lots of forsythia left. If you stripped the stems and just left a few delicate blossoms on the ends you could work some in."

"And create a harmony!" I said.

"Exactly."

Once I'd seen below the surface I realised Celia was very nice. We worked alongside each other, both offering encouragement. Her finished arrangement was stunning and mine at least looked as though I'd tried.

As we cleared up we were reminded to vote for our favourite arrangements. Admittedly I'm no expert, but they all looked good to me. The lady opposite me had made a massive bouquet thing of bright tulips, anemones and coloured foliage. It wasn't at all sophisticated, but it was fun. Guessing she wouldn't get many votes, but any she did get would mean a lot, I put her entry number down on my voting slip.

We had to leave for the formal judging then, so I nipped to the pub for an orange juice. Not my usual tipple, but I was driving. I only just made it back in time to hear the results.

Third place and then second were called. The entrants all clapped as the certificates were handed out. The helpful woman wasn't called, so I was hoping she'd won.

"And now it gives me great pleasure to announce that the grand prize winner… is… Hannah Goodyear."

Celia gasped. "That can't be right."

The helpful woman looked just as shocked. Could she be Hannah, I wondered.

The other entrants began to congratulate 'Celia' and push her towards the stage, saying, 'Well done, Hannah."

Celia wasn't Celia at all!

Fortunately my sister phoned just then, demanding to know the result. I told her, explained my confusion and described the helpful woman.

"That's Celia," Freya told me. "She isn't really helpful. She pretends to be, but just gives people doubts. She does things like suggesting a little yellow would really lift a display and she'll be right, but she'll only mention it when that's the one colour bloom you don't have."

"Or suggest feathery foliage when only big leaves are available?"

"Exactly." Her agreement was almost drowned out by clapping. "What's happening now?" she asked.

"The entrants' choice award."

"Who got that?"

"Listen," I said as I heard my name. Everyone clapped and congratulated me, even the real Celia. Maybe my theory about competition stress making her unkind had some truth in it after all?

"Chris Clarke, are you here?" the judge called again.

I was pushed forward to collect my award.

"I don't believe it!" Freya screeched in my ear when she called back a few minutes later.

"Why not? You said I'd be good at this."

"Only to get you to come to classes."

"Why did you want me to?"

"Because, brother dear, you and Hannah are perfect for each other."

I was tempted to say if she was right that would make it an 'arranged marriage'. Instead I ended the call and invited Hannah to dinner.

13. The Tree Within

"Are you sure there's not a tree growing in there?" Joshua placed his hand on Kate's bump as she crunched through an apple.

She just grinned at her husband and finished the sweet juicy piece of fruit, core and all. She'd always eaten them that way, though usually only when alone.

Years ago, fellow schoolchildren had teased that the pips would grow inside her. Grandad used to give her home-grown apples; he'd stored them carefully so they lasted right through to spring and every bite of every one was precious. It seemed wasteful not to eat the core when it tasted just as good as the rest. Besides it couldn't be right about the pips. No one worried about seeds in the granary bread their sandwiches were made of or nuts in chocolate bars. Even so Kate had either eaten her apples away from everyone else or, when that wasn't possible, had regretfully discarded the core. Wanting to please others, Kate tried to behave as people expected. She'd hidden more than her habit of eating apple cores.

In drama class, the children were told to act like trees. Kate stood completely still and imagined how it would feel to have sap rising, birds nesting, fruit swelling. It would be wonderful. Trees were lovely. She'd like to be one. She'd planted her feet solidly on the ground and stretched her limbs up, up, up towards where she imagined the sun to be, wishing she could feel its early spring warmth and the breath of the wind on her skin.

"Come on girl, don't just stand there," the teacher said.

Kate had opened her eyes and seen the other children thrashing about. They looked nothing like trees, but apparently that was what the teacher wanted so Kate ran haphazardly, leaping and twisting.

"Much better," the teacher said.

"Perhaps she thought I looked like driftwood caught in a torrent?" she asked Grandad later.

He got her to demonstrate both versions and confirmed her opinion that the first was far more realistic.

"Too wooden for your teacher, I expect," he chuckled.

"Is that bad?"

"Nothing about my little sapling is bad," he'd told her, ruffling her hair.

He thought of her as a tree! Nothing could have pleased her more. He was definitely a tree to her. A magnificent oak perhaps, or gnarled and character filled beech. Something solid, reliable, sheltering and wonderful. All her life she'd tried to follow his example.

Recently Kate had gone public with her apple core crunching. Pregnant women were expected to eat unusual things and though some made the same silly joke about the pips her husband had, they did so kindly.

"You'll be wanting to call her Willow or Hazel, I suppose," Joshua said.

"I thought Rowan. That's appropriate for another branch on our family tree."

Joshua smiled. "Any child of yours will be a whole tree, just like her mother."

"You think of me as a tree?"

"In a good way, I promise."

"There is no other."

She'd done her best, always. After losing Grandad, she'd felt like that piece of driftwood she'd enacted at school. Then she'd met Joshua and put down roots. Now she was nurturing a new life. She'd be there for as long as she was able, to shelter and protect their daughter. Like Grandad had done for her.

Like a tree.

14. Winter Garden

"Come on then, tell me what's wrong." Imogen invited, as they waited for the cheerful waitress to bring their tea and scones.

"I already have – probably too many times!" Imogen was the first person Stacey had called when she got the news of her redundancy from the accountancy firm, after almost twenty years. Imogen had given her a much needed hug and words of sympathy when it happened and in the months since.

"I wanted to be sure it was just about losing your job, nothing new."

"Isn't that enough?"

"To be honest, I don't understand why you're quite so down about it. You never even liked that job."

Stacey felt herself smile. She was so glad Imogen had talked her into coming out for the day. Her friend could always make her see the bright side. "I wasn't keen on being cooped up when I'd rather be in the fresh air, but my colleagues were a friendly bunch and I liked the money!"

Imogen gave a frown. "Are you not getting the payout you expected?"

"It's already in the bank."

"You've got enough to live on? I thought you worked all that out."

"I did, yes. I won't lose the house or go hungry. A lot of people aren't so lucky, nowhere near. I should be grateful, but somehow I'm not."

"Come on then, tell me what's really wrong."

"I'm just fed up. At first I enjoyed having free time, but once I'd got my garden perfect, and the novelty of two hour lunch breaks wore off, I started feeling sorry for myself. Sometimes it feels my whole life was a mistake! Getting pregnant at sixteen, marrying Nat because of it and not making that work. Neglecting my daughter to study, then neglecting her as I worked hard and got promoted and it's all been for nothing."

Imogen reached across and put a comforting hand on Stacey's arm. "No it hasn't, silly. You did a brilliant job raising Jinny."

"With a lot of help from you." Stacey grinned.

"Well, she is my goddaughter."

"Choosing you was something I got right."

"And as a good godmother, don't you think I'd have said something if you'd neglected her?"

"You're right, even if I wasn't always there she wasn't neglected."

"And your determined, hard working example has produced a happy, delightful young woman with the confidence to branch out and create exactly the life she wants for herself. Your sacrifices made that possible." Imogen chuckled. "Of course my good influence helped a lot."

"Of course it did. Thank you." Stacey got up and hugged her friend.

Imogen looked thoughtful as they poured tea, and spread generous quantities of jam and cream onto their scones.

"Do you remember that garden we went to on your birthday last year?" Imogen asked. "I'd read about all the colour and how well tended it was, so thought you'd love it, but when we arrived it seemed the plants and staff had just given up."

"Yes, but… What are you saying? I should do the equivalent of buying some bedding plants to cheer myself up? Sorry, but I've already redone every pot I have and my courtyard garden isn't big enough to accommodate any more retail therapy."

"No, that's not what I'm saying at all. Let's visit the garden again – my treat."

"That's a nice thought." It was, just as it had been when she'd suggested it last July. Beyond that first rather disappointing area they'd discovered a rose garden in full glory, a lake surrounded by a woodland walk, plus a picnic area with beds of bright annuals – and a kiosk which not only sold fab food but also loaned out blankets so visitors could picnic on the lawn.

"You don't sound convinced," Imogen said.

"I am about it being nice of you to suggest it, but it's not going to be looking like much in February, is it?"

"You're the one who's always saying there's more to gardens than pretty flowers. There's form and structure and mulch, whatever that is."

Stacey laughed. "Oh dear, do I lecture?"

"Hardly at all, besides I never listen!"

Stacey knew the second part wasn't true. Her friend always listened and often helped. She was helping now. "OK, you've talked me into it. If nothing else, the walk will do me good – especially after eating these scones."

"That's the spirit."

After paying to enter the garden, Imogen grabbed a leaflet and marched straight to the part of the garden she'd previously said looked neglected. Nobody would think that now. There were pools and rivers of brilliant colour all weaving their way between fat clumps of early hellebores and swathes of pristine snowdrops.

"Wow!" Stacey said.

"My sentiments exactly. Are these all real flowers?"

"Oh yes. I grow some of them in my pots at home. Although they don't look so impressive on a small scale it's still cheery to have colour at this time of year."

"What are those bright magenta ones? They look like that lovely cyclamen you gave me for Christmas."

"That's exactly what they are, although hardy ones, not the hothouse type you have."

"Had. I think I've killed it already!"

"Poor thing. And to think I let you babysit my child! Oooh, look at those aconites." She crouched down to inspect the tiny, golden yellow cup shaped flowers, surrounded by a ruff of bright green leaves. "I wish I could grow these, but they need very different conditions than I can provide."

"You've got some of those blue and purple ones, haven't you?"

"The iris? Yes."

"I thought iris were a summer flower?"

"There are summer flowering kinds. Those have rhizomes rather than bulbs though. These are reticulata… Ooops, sorry – lecturing again! Don't they look good against the cornus stems?" She pointed to where brilliant red and flaming orange stems glowed in the low sun.

"They do. And something smells good too."

"That's winter honeysuckle, I think. Yes, look there's a plant." As they walked on other scents wafted out. Delicate mahonia, the rich and slightly sharp aroma of witch hazel, deliciously sweet daphne.

The dark leaves of black grass edged the path, contrasting with golden gravel, the brightly coloured flowers and the ghostly stems of silver birch and white stemmed bramble. It was fabulous. For a time Stacey was too entranced by the gorgeous winter garden to think of anything else, but gradually she realised Imogen had brought her there for a reason – something more than the distraction of pretty flowers.

"You're saying things might look better for me if I wait for the right moment?" Stacey asked. "Sort of." Imogen held out the leaflet she'd picked up. Rather than the map Stacey had assumed, it was an advertisement for an assistant gardener. Full training to be provided. "You could do that."

"I'd love it!"

"And you'd be good at it if you got it."

"Yes, I… Hey! You knew about this vacancy and got me here on purpose, didn't you?"

"I had heard about it, yes. You might not get it though," she cautioned.

"True, but I won't know if I don't try. And if it's a no, there will be other jobs I can apply for. Other things I could do." Her life so far hadn't been a waste. As Imogen had said, she'd done a good job raising her daughter. Now it was Stacey's turn to bloom.

15. Green Fingered Grandad

Every year, Grandad wins prizes at the village show for his flowers and vegetables. Mummy says I should be proud, but I'm not because he cheats.

"He must have green fingers," everyone says. "Couldn't grow stuff like that without."

It's not true. That's how I know he cheats. His fingers are as pink as mine and his gloves are blue.

16. A Blooming Mystery

Each time Maria stepped into her front garden, she was greeted by a wonderful display of pastel flowers. There were godetia and clarkia in a restrained mix of pinks and whites, standing proud with their backs to the house. Just in front were groups of stocks in the same shades as well as a soft mauve. These added a lovely perfume to the display.

Between each patch of stocks was one of airy annual gypsophila. Those and the gently contrasting baby blue eyes, which grew at their feet, almost gave the impression that the summer sky was woven into the planting scheme.

Throughout it all, giving a much stronger contrast and providing real impact was a bold arc of towering cosmos in a rich, deep shade of burgundy. Those final flowers turned the pretty scene into a truly beautiful one.

"It looks fabulous," neighbours remarked.

Complete strangers stopped to look, comment and praise as they walked by Maria's corner plot. Some asked if they might take photographs. Somebody had even written to the local paper, suggesting that readers 'do yourself a favour and take a walk down to where Blackbird Avenue meets Goldfinch Crescent. You won't be disappointed!'

All those flowers were wonderful, but Maria's delight wasn't complete. The cosmos were a real puzzle.

Maria allowed herself to enjoy the compliments. She had done the work. The digging and addition of compost. The raking and sowing, watering and feeding. Every day she checked for litter blown in and carefully removed any she saw with a special gadget which allowed her to reach right into the border without stepping on the soil.

And she'd done all the planning. Almost all of it anyway. Maria had studied seed catalogues to select the right strains of the right varieties of flowers, and ordered them in good time. She'd drawn a plan to show where most of them would be positioned. Not the cosmos though. Maria had chosen it as being healthy and vigorous, with delicate ferny foliage. It was just the right tone of burgundy to set off the white, blue pink and mauve of the other blooms. The rich, deep colour and wonderfully velvety texture of the petals added something magical, but it wasn't marked on her planting plan and very nearly wasn't used at all. Without the cosmos, her garden would still look very nice but it wouldn't be so wonderful that people took a detour just to see it.

Maria wanted to explain that something had mysteriously come to her aid, but knew how odd that would sound. She worried about other people's opinions of her far more than she should.

"Maria!" Lara called, startling her a little. "I'm glad to have caught you at last. Somehow I keep missing you."

That was because Maria had been avoiding her friend.

"I have to compliment you on this triumph." Lara gestured to Maria's blossom filled garden. "It always looks good, but those cosmos are a stroke of genius!"

Those words were the reason Maria had avoided Lara. To her friend she couldn't pretend she'd not had that mysterious help. And that meant admitting the whole thing didn't just sound odd, but really was.

"I owe you an apology. I doubted you'd be brave enough," Lara continued.

"Oh, but I wasn't! I don't know how this happened."

"You didn't do this?"

"No. Well of course I planted it, but not... I did everything exactly as usual. Safe." Maria whispered the last word.

A year previously, she and Lara had been standing in the garden, with Maria enjoying compliments about her well tended blooms, when she'd heard someone murmur, 'pretty, but it's all so predictable, so safe.'

"What did she mean?" Maria had asked her friend after the woman had moved on.

"Don't take any notice. You work so hard to make your garden look nice and most people appreciate the result."

"That's true, but I'd still like to know what she meant," Maria said.

"Well... You select only pastel blooms, and plant seeds carefully so the tallest plants are at the back, dropping neatly down to the front."

Maria had felt a little defensive and explained that was so they'd co-ordinate and as many flowers as possible were clearly visible. It was the usual, traditional way to do it.

"Quite so, and as so many people have been telling you it looks very pretty. But you must admit, it is safe," Lara said.

"You think I should do something dangerous?"

"No, but perhaps just slightly daring? A bolder colour, or a taller plant in the middle, something like that."

Maria now explained that she'd tried to follow Lara's advice. "I bought the dark cosmos seeds as well as my usual selection..."

"They were a great choice."

"Seeing them in bloom, I agree, but in the spring I lost my nerve and never sowed them."

"What? But…" Lara sounded as confused and Maria had been feeling ever since the seedlings had emerged.

"I know."

"Tell me precisely what happened."

"I ordered the seed and prepared the ground as usual. I made out my planting plan, but didn't include the cosmos as I couldn't decide what to do with them."

"OK. And then, when you came to plant… ?"

"I stood in the garden and wished aloud for help, for confidence perhaps, or inspiration. A large flock of birds swooped down to the feeding station and I considered sowing my seeds in drifts, rather than precisely placed little blocks. But then a single magpie hopped past."

"One for sorrow," Lara said.

"I'm not really superstitious, but I decided against the drifts." Maria continued, "Butterflies danced in the air and I thought of mingling all the seeds together for a naturalistic look. I couldn't do that either."

"I can see that. Random abandonment isn't your thing! Go on."

"I snipped open all the foil packs and then arranged everything just as usual. I thought about putting a few cosmos right at the back. That would have added the extra colour without a big break from my usual approach."

"A good compromise. Why didn't you?"

"When I came to do it the seeds were missing. The cosmos look wonderful just as they are, but I'm not responsible and have no idea how they got there."

"This is worrying you, isn't it?"

Maria admitted it was. Then seeing that her friend was trying hard to think of a solution, she silently offered her a toffee from the pack in her pocket.

As Lara took one, an empty wrapper came out too and fluttered down onto a flower bed. Maria resisted the temptation to run in for her long handled gadget to pick it up. That could wait a few minutes.

"You say you asked for help?" Lara asked.

"Yes."

"Then someone must have given it. Who was around?"

"Absolutely nobody. It was just me, the birds and butterflies."

"The seeds must have got scattered by the wind."

"I'd chosen a really still day. I always do."

"Then there's only one explanation!"

"Which is?"

Lara put a finger to her lips and pointed to where a magpie had landed in the flower bed and was hopping towards the shiny sweet wrapper.

"He picked up the pack and as he flew away the seeds spilled out in that wide arc," Maria immediately realised. It was an odd thing to happen, but she wasn't responsible. Not that year anyway. Next year she would do something similar, but so as not to be too safe, too predictable, she'd choose a different accent plant. Deep blue larkspur perhaps, or mahogany marigolds, brilliant white mallows…

17. Endless Adventures

As Anna waved her granddaughter Lily and her little boys Tomas and Jacob off, she felt guilty. The visits were often the highlight of her week, but was she being fair to allow them to continue? It must be so boring for the boys.

Anna had tried to say something when Lily and her family first moved in nearby and it was suggested that she call in on her way to and from the supermarket each week. "It's practically on my way, and I can pick up any shopping you can't get from the corner shop, or which is too heavy to carry."

"That's very kind, but it must be hard enough doing your own shopping with these two. You don't want to be doing mine as well."

"What about if I left them with you, Gran?"

Both boys had looked pleased with the suggestion, and Anna was delighted. She remembered spending time with her Grandad and enjoying every moment of the wonderful adventures he arranged for them. If she could entertain Tomas and Jacob, she'd be returning the favour Lily was doing her as well as having a nice time herself.

At first it had been wonderful. The help with the shopping was appreciated, as were the little jobs Lily sometimes did around the house. She thought nothing of changing a lightbulb or fixing a dripping tap, and did those things whilst continuing to chat. The best part though were those conversations, and time, spent with Tomas and Jacob. The arrangement had begun in late autumn, and the weather was often fine enough to take them to the little park which was just a few minutes walk away. By the time they'd fed the ducks, had a go on the swings and slide and gone back to Anna's for a snack their mother would arrive to collect them.

Just as the novelty of doing that every week was wearing off, winter closed in. As the boys couldn't get out and play much anyway, Anna didn't feel bad that it was her house they were cooped up in. And of course the house itself was another novelty for them. They were easily kept occupied for an hour or so each week looking at her paintings, ornaments and old photo albums. Anna told them stories about the different people in the pictures, or who'd given her which trinket.

Once those options were all exhausted, Anna asked Lily to fetch down a box of books from the attic. To Tomas and Jacob, she read adventure stories which had first belonged to her children, then her grandchildren. Over Christmas they made paper chains and cards, decorated the tree and later wrote thank you letters for gifts they'd received. That break meant the story books lasted well into the New Year, but they'd all been read long before the arrival of sunny spring weather.

On their next visit, unless she got a brilliant idea, Anna would have to resort to sitting the boys in front of the television. There wasn't anything wrong with that of course – except that's what Lily often did, so she could get on with housework, and the book keeping she did part time. Anna wanted the boys to be engaged and stimulated, just as she and her siblings had been as children.

It wasn't so easy these days. When Anna was little, children were often sent out to play unsupervised. She'd had three older brothers and a sister which made that reasonably safe, and allowed for quite complicated games. Anna had to keep Tomas and Jacob within sight at all times, which meant they couldn't run about more than she could herself. Like her legs, Anna's pension didn't always go quite as far as she'd have liked, so she couldn't buy them exciting toys and games… but then neither could her grandad do that for all his grandchildren. He hadn't run about much either. In fact he'd seemed to spend most of his time in the pigeon loft – so how exactly had he taken her and her brothers and sister on so many adventures?

They'd usually started with the children all being given costumes, Anna recalled. He wouldn't have bought those, and it was impossible to imagine Grandad sewing. Anna could picture him with scissors though… Huge great red handled scissors which he used to cut up the sacks which had held the corn he fed his pigeons on. That was it! He'd just cut holes for their head and legs, and said it was a princess's dress, Roman tunic, hero's cape or whatever else would suit the game they were to play.

Sometimes a cut off corner was a hat and Anna and her siblings were Robin Hood and his merry men. Grandad even made them bows and arrows from bendy sticks and string. Gosh, you couldn't do that these days! Health and Safety people would have fits! And those same bows and arrows had been used to play Cowboys and Indians. It was the political correctness people who'd have fits over that. Quite right too. They'd meant no harm or disrespect at the time, but knew better now. What else had they played? The sacks had been monk's outfits sometimes, but she couldn't think now what game they'd managed to come up with. It probably involved chanting. They'd loved to sing, even though they rarely recalled the words and couldn't always hang on to the tune.

One thing the games all had in common was a lot of imagination – and almost nothing else. Grandad didn't spend any money, and once he'd set them off on their games he'd gone back to doing whatever it was he did with the pigeons. She could hardly let her little great grandsons out to play on the streets all alone these days, but perhaps her imagination was still in working order?

Of course it was. When explaining what was happening in decades old photos of family groups, quite often she'd forgotten some of the details and either made them up or invited the boys to do so. That was fun. Often she, Tomas and Jacob had used the illustrations in the adventure story books to extend and embellish the original tales. If she could only come up with an idea, and perhaps a few props, she was sure the boys' imaginations could be relied on to aid hers and make up entertaining games.

What would Grandad do if he were here now? For a start, he'd make use of what was to hand – Anna's house and garden, and the things within it. That thought cheered her, as she'd done that already to some extent. She just needed to take it a stage further. Right down the garden to where the earliest spring bulbs were just putting in an appearance…

It was an incredibly cold day when Lily next brought the boys over, but it was dry so they could go outside if they all dressed warmly. Lily was hardly out the door when Anna produced a pile of hats gloves and scarves.

"Where are we going, Granny?" Tomas asked.

"To the ends of the earth!"

"Why?" Jacob wanted to know. Tomas was more interested in whether that was a really long way.

"It's ever such a long way and we're going because we're intrepid plant hunters."

"What's a trepid plant hunter?"

"They go to faraway lands and bring back plants people have never seen before. When my grandad was little, people hardly ever saw bananas and oranges, and we didn't have so many flowers and things in our gardens, so explorers had to find them."

"Mummy goes to the supermarket and gets them now," Tomas pointed out.

Anna thought for a moment. What had her brothers liked searching for? Ah yes, she remembered. "We're not looking for oranges, but treasure!"

That did the trick, and the boys put on some of the gloves and things themselves, and wrapped Anna in several scarves.

"The first thing we must do is sail across the sea," Anna explained. The boys seemed to have doubts as they boarded the boat, OK the hall carpet, but they all sat down in a row and rocked side to side, just as Anna's youngest daughter had taught her to do to some pop song once. As she couldn't remember how that went, Anna had them singing, 'Row, row your boat' instead.

"Can you see a seagull?" she asked once the song ended.

"I can!" Tomas exclaimed, pointing to one of her china ornaments. It actually looked like a slightly faded robin, unless you were an intrepid plant and treasure hunter who knew better.

"Pirate ship!" Jacob warned, gesturing to the curtain, moving slightly in a draft.

"Row faster," Anna urged. Then recalling they had no oars, sent Tomas to fetch her wooden spoons. Bless him, he pretended to swim as he did that.

Just as they got away from the dastardly pirates, they were chased by a huge octopus. Fortunately the hallway table with all its cables for the telephone, answering machine and lamp was a friendly creature. Once it caught them, instead of setting about them with wiring tentacles, it told silly jokes.

Where do sharks go on holiday? Finland! What happened to the minnow who got famous? He became a star fish! Why don't crabs share their sweets? They're too shellfish!

Soon they were hot in all their extra woollen accessories and Anna decided it was time to move on.

"We need to get our supplies ashore," she said. Which the boys did by hauling her to her feet.

They climbed the mountain, OK the stairs, for a good vantage point over the strange new land of Anna's back garden, just emerging from its winter sleep.

"I think I can see the treasure," Anna said. She led them back down the mountain, out across the wilderness of her patio, and through the forest of two heavily pruned rose bushes and a spotted laurel. She'd never been quite sure she liked that, but kept it as at least it was something to look at in winter. It was also, she learned from Tomas, a good place for bears to hide, so they had to creep by quietly.

Finally at the end of a long trail, beside a cave where a strange creature lived and just before they got to the wheelie bins, they discovered precious metals and jewels sprinkled on the ground. There was the gold of the last winter aconites, amethyst and garnet crocus, snowdrop pearls and huge rubies of peony snouts just starting to brave the cold.

"Can we collect some treasure for Mummy?" the boys asked.

Anna agreed they could, but it wouldn't be easy! "First we need something to keep them safe, during our long journey home." That involved stealthily gathering leaves from the spotted laurel, without disturbing the bear, and then a framework of coloured twigs from all corners of the garden – including those guarded by the ferocious whatdoyoucallit, which to the untrained eye looked like a rotary washing line. Luckily Anna knew better and was able to advise Tomas and Jacob to perform the magic spell of running around it once backwards and three times forward, which allowed them to pass unharmed.

The boys picked snowdrops, to add to the leaf and twig posey, and managed to take it safely past most of the obstacles before their mother returned to collect them. She didn't mind waiting while they sailed the hall carpet back, was amused by a few more of the octopus' jokes, and was delighted with her flowers.

Tomas asked, "Are the jewels worth lots and lots of money?"

"Not these ones," Anna admitted. Imagination was one thing, but she wasn't going to lie. "But in the olden days, the plants the explorers found were worth a fortune." She told the boys how years and years ago people used to trade in tulips, sometimes selling one single dry bulb for the price of a house.

"Have you got any of those?" Tomas asked.

"We'll have to do a search one day, and find out, won't we?"

"I can't wait!" Jacob declared.

Neither could Anna. And they wouldn't have to. In the weeks before the tulips would be in bloom they could explore the strange cave Tomas had spotted, right by where her shed was located, and the enchanted grotto, which was also her rockery. With a bit of imagination, the possibilities for adventure were endless.

18. Company For Robert

The three of us sat in the outside space behind the office. There's just room for a tiny table, our chairs and a pot of bright flowers. It's not grand, but it does catch the early evening sun.

"Robert was probably amazed you had the nerve to divorce him, Anne."

Julie, Louisa and I were discussing recent changes to my life over a celebratory bottle of sparkling wine. Julie and I had become business partners and Louisa was our first full-time employee.

"It's his own fault. He thought he could do what he liked because he's so irresistible to women."

Julie and I laughed. We knew all about Robert's apparent romantic success.

"Usual thing, he left me for a younger woman," I explained to Louisa. "He came crawling back when the latest girl said she didn't want him. She liked the dinners in restaurants, the nice presents, the flowers, flattery and seduction. She didn't want to cook for him or iron his shirts. She wouldn't sit at home on her own whilst he went drinking with his mates. She stood up to him. Maybe if I'd done that our marriage would have survived, who knows?"

"Sounds as though you're better off without him," Louisa said.

"He wasn't worthy of you," Julie added.

"Thanks. I happen to think you're right. He came back home; my home now. He didn't like it when I said I didn't want him either. He'd tried to throw me out but I'd gone to a solicitor and found out what I was entitled to."

"Yes, I remember, he claimed that as you hadn't worked everything was his," Julie said.

The phone rang and interrupted us. Louisa jumped up to answer it.

"It's OK. I'll go, you stay and learn the company history," Julie said.

"Robert didn't like me to work. I'd lost touch with most of my friends. Robert didn't exactly encourage me to spend time with them. Eventually I had nothing in my life except him. No wonder he got bored with me."

"So you were on your own and looking for work?"

"Yes. Once he left I had to do something to fill my time. Otherwise I'd have given in to depression. I tracked Julie down, and tried to contact some of my other old school friends."

"Sorry I didn't contact you back then. We'd all had such ambitious plans and I felt such a failure that I couldn't face meeting up with you," Louisa said.

"You're not a failure." I assured her and squeezed her hand. "It's just that, like most people, your life didn't go the way you'd thought it would when you were a kid."

"Had the others changed much?" Louisa aske.

"It was a comfort in a way to find that they'd not all made a wonderful success of everything. Some were happy enough, but if they had a good marriage and family they didn't have the glittering career they'd planned. Those whose work life was going well were single or struggling to hold a relationship together. One was suffering from a serious illness. Thankfully she had the loving support of her family. I began to realise that most people don't 'have it all.'"

"I suppose you're right." She poured more bubbly into my glass.

"Julie was doing well though. She'd just started this business and offered me a job. I didn't take it then, but her offer gave me the confidence to start sorting myself out. I'd not driven the car much. Robert's comments made me nervous. I booked refresher lessons and found that after some practice my confidence and ability grew. I worked out a budget. It was hard, but I didn't have the electricity cut off. A light bulb blew. I bought a new one, got out the step ladders and replaced it. It doesn't sound like much, but to me that was a sign I could cope alone."

"You've done more than cope." It was Louisa's turn to reassure me. "What did you do next?"

"The garden. Robert's pet project. If he wasn't down the pub he was tinkering with his ferns and hostas. I bought a small electric lawnmower. The petrol model Robert insisted on was difficult to start and difficult to handle. I cut the grass in half the time it used to take him. I admired the bright flowers the neighbours grew, which Robert thought were common, and bought myself some. It isn't Kew Gardens but it's neat and cheerful. Some neighbours walking by stopped when they saw me with the watering can and said how pretty it looks."

Julie came back. "Another booking. A big corporate hospitality thing."

"Can we do that?" I asked.

"Yes, it's not for a few weeks. Where had you got to, then?"

"Anne was just saying how her neighbours admired her garden," Louisa explained.

"They were right; it's lovely. When I saw how well she ran the house and garden I knew she'd be an asset with the business."

I grinned, remembering how Julie's praise had provided much needed confidence.

"My few successes convinced me I wasn't guaranteed to fail at everything. When Julie said she wanted to discuss a business venture I was ready for a challenge. Having started the company she didn't want to lose it, even though her pregnancy meant she couldn't put in enough hours. Just as we've done with you, she suggested I start part time and learn on the job."

"That plan has worked out well for all of us," Louisa says. "I still don't understand how Robert got his come-uppance though?"

"We'll need more wine for that story. Good thing we weren't planning on driving home." Julie went to fetch a second bottle.

"I began visiting local pubs, clubs and restaurants so we could recommend suitable places to clients. Robert seemed to appear wherever I went. Each time he was with a different girl. Each time he would bring her to speak to me."

"Maybe he just wanted to prove that although you were alone, he was not?"

"That's what I thought, so was polite to them all. Why should I feel jealous because a young, slim girl was eating out at his expense? Julie had little Jason by then and I'd taken over most of the management. I wasn't the insecure wife he remembered. I found I had a talent for working with people. Both the staff and customers trust me. Well, one day I saw Robert alone. 'Have you run out of girlfriends then?' I asked him. 'They seem to get fed up with you pretty quickly.' The next time I saw him he didn't introduce me to his companion. I saw them together a few more times. Eventually he introduced her to me as his fiancée. She looked uncomfortable and wore no ring. I just shrugged and walked away. When she went to the toilet I followed. She explained the true situation to me; they weren't engaged at all. She'd been as surprised as me when he said they were."

Julie came back again and started removing the foil from the bottle. "Go on Anne, this is the best bit."

"I went over and asked him how they'd met, then said 'It's OK I already know. You booked her with my new company, Julie-Anne's escort agency.'"

Julie eased out the cork and refilled our glasses.

19. A Gift From The Past

Eva took the coat off the rack in the charity shop. It was in her favourite shade of soft turquoise, seemed to be new, and looked just the right weight for what she wanted. It was oddly familiar, but she was sure she'd not seen any of her friends or neighbours wearing it. She slipped it on.

Tomorrow would be her and Tom's forty-eighth wedding anniversary and they were celebrating with a picnic in the park by their special bench. The picnic would be special too. Their daughters and daughters-in-law were preparing the food and drink which would be shared with them, their partners and children.

Eva had treated herself to a new dress for the occasion. The material was in a bold pattern of turquoise, grey and white. The neckline was high with a white collar. The hemline was quite high too, just skimming her knees. It was the kind of dress which was very popular in the sixties among girls confident enough to wear them. Eva hadn't been one of those then, not until she met Tom.

The turquoise coat fitted perfectly. Thanks to their daily walks, Eva still had a trim figure, and good legs. The coat didn't hide those, but would give a little warmth should the promised spring sunshine not be quite enough once she was sitting still.

"That really suits you," the assistant said. "Come and look in the mirror." She opened the changing room door, inviting Eva to go in.

As she walked towards the mirror Eva gasped. She knew where she'd seen the coat before! Somehow finding it today felt like a gift from the past.

"I'll take it," Eva said. "I don't suppose you have a scarf in that same colour do you?"

"We might do."

The two women examined the extensive selection of scarves. There were some nice ones, but none matching the coat. "Don't worry, it was just an idea," Eva said.

Making her way back to the tearoom where she and Tom were to meet she thought back to when she'd first seen the coat. Or rather one very like it. That was over forty years ago – it couldn't be the same one.

Eva had been working for the council then. The office in which she worked had a view of a small public garden. As she was too shy to start conversations with her colleagues she often went to gaze out the window during tea breaks. Most mornings she'd seen a lady walking along the circular path. Eva chuckled to herself. The lady had seemed elderly to her younger self, but had probably only been the same age she was now. Seventy-six wasn't old these days. Nobody had looked surprised when she and Tom took their grandchildren roller skating, booked a hiking tour or enrolled in Tai Chi classes.

Young Eva though had seen the lady in the turquoise coat regularly pause in about the same spot and thought she must be tired. It occurred to her that this would be an excellent position for a bench on which the lady could rest. As the small garden was owned by the council and her office was very close to the department who administered parks and gardens Eva was in the perfect position to suggest it. There was even a nice young man in that department who often said good morning to her. She could mention it to him – if she could only find the nerve.

She continued to watch the lady, who walked by at roughly the same time each day. Soon Eva noticed a gentleman quite often walked round in the opposite direction. Each of them was always quite alone. She only rarely saw them pass, but when they did it seemed as though they acknowledged each other. Young Eva had thought how nice it would be if they were to become friends. If there was a bench it would help with that, as it would be natural for them to sit for a while. Eventually they'd do so at the same time and strike up a conversation and from that small beginning, build a relationship. She could make it happen. Eva left her desk, walked out of the office and turned towards the parks and gardens department.

"Off to see Tom Watkins are you, Eva?" a colleague who was returning from the lavatories asked.

"No, no. Of course not," she mumbled.

"Why not? We've all seen that you like him."

Eva had been mortified and fled back to her desk.

Her colleague had followed. "I'm sorry, lovey. I was only teasing."

"What's wrong, Eva?" her supervisor asked.

"It was my fault. I thought she and Tom Watkins might have got together at last."

"Leave the poor lass be," the supervisor said.

They all got back to work and Eva tried to forget about it, but several times she heard snatches of conversation she thought might be about her and Tom Watkins. Often these included phrases such as 'they'd be perfect together' and 'need a push in the right direction'.

A week later, when Eva looked down on the little garden she saw the gentleman walk by wearing a scarf in the exact shade of soft turquoise as the lady's coat. All the words she'd heard said about her filled Eva's mind. She was sure both the gentleman and the lady were lonely and could bring each other happiness. She simply couldn't let her shyness stand in the way of that!

By the time Eva reached Tom's desk her legs were shaking and her words bubbled out in a confused torrent. Thankfully he seemed to understand at least some of it and said he'd speak to his supervisor. An hour later he came to ask if she would show him the spot where she felt the bench should be sited.

When they reached the location, Eva saw that it was even more perfect than she'd realised. It was the one spot in the garden where the view wouldn't be of the overlooking buildings, but of a small pond and the trees behind.

The day work to instal the bench began, Eva saw the older couple stop to talk – about the new bench she was sure. As she'd hoped, they sat there together quite often in the following weeks and months.

They weren't the only people to use the bench of course. Young mothers stopped to gossip as they gently rocked their prams. People sat to read newspapers or books in the sun. And Tom and Eva sat together to eat their lunchtime sandwiches. Over forty years later they still did so occasionally, which was why they'd chosen the spot as the location for their anniversary celebration.

Eva joined Tom in the tearoom where they'd agreed to meet. "I hope I haven't kept you waiting. I got rather lost in thought and probably dawdled."

"I was a bit late myself," Tom admitted. "It took me a while to find what I wanted."

"I hope you haven't bought me an anniversary present. We agreed not to do that."

"Don't worry, Eva love, this is for me. Not that I need any kind of gift beyond the one I was given all those years ago when you marched up to my desk and babbled about a man in a turquoise scarf and a lady needing a bench. But somehow it seemed right to get this for tomorrow." He placed a small bag on the table.

Eva pulled out a scarf in their favourite shade of soft turquoise.

20. That Damned Cat!

"That damned cat!" Harry muttered.

The rotten thing had made his life hell for months. It scratched in his garden so often he'd given up trying to plant anything. He'd stopped feeding the birds too – he'd be luring them to their deaths. He didn't go outside much, because whenever he did the cat would wind itself round his legs, putting him at serious risk of falling.

"Put a sock in it!" Harry yelled as the cat yowled again.

Because of the cat, Harry hadn't got to know his new neighbour. Better to keep out of her way he thought, than cause offence by showing his opinion of her horrible pet. One way or another it had made Harry lonely, grumpy, and feeling much older than his fifty-five years. Now it wouldn't shut up and let him concentrate on the crossword.

"Can't a man be allowed a bit of peace in his own home?" He threw down his paper. "Now the blasted thing has got me talking to myself," he muttered.

He hauled himself out of his chair, opened the window and was trying to decide whether to yell at it or throw something, when a thought struck him. If he could hear the cat when it was next door and he had his window shut, his neighbour could surely hear it making a racket right outside her back door. Her kitchen window was on the latch. Not open enough for the cat to get in, just enough to let out the steam if she'd been cooking.

By the noise it was making you'd think the thing was in dreadful pain, but as it paced round and round on the mat

Harry could see no sign of injury. Annoying as the dratted animal was, it was usually quiet. If his neighbour would just let it in then it would shut up. He couldn't think why she didn't. Well, if she wouldn't, he would!

Harry kicked off his slippers, pulled on his shoes and stomped down his front path. He walked briskly up his neighbour's path. It was dawning on him something was wrong. He rang her doorbell, but didn't stop to see if she'd answer. If she could hear it ring and open the front door, she'd have heard her cat and opened the back one. A quick try of the handle showed him the front door was locked.

"Hello!" he called as he strode down the passage.

No reply, except from the cat.

Harry rattled the back door handle. Locked. He looked in the window and saw his neighbour slumped on the floor with something red and sticky dripping down her chest.

"Hello! Hello!"

No response. Even the cat was quiet.

He rushed back home and called the ambulance, cursing the fact he'd stopped bothering to charge his mobile. After giving as much information as he could, Harry said, "I'm going back now, to see if I can get in and help."

Harry couldn't force the window open, or find a key hidden under a pot or the mat. A squint through the lock showed the key was in it. He picked up the smallest of her plant pots and gently tipped out the pink begonia. Using the pot as a kind of glove, he smashed one small glass panel of her door, reached inside and turned the key.

"I'm Harry from next door," he said. "I'm a trained first aider and I'm here to help." He knew that often people could hear even when they couldn't react, and it was important to reassure and explain, not just start touching them when they were vulnerable. Not that it really mattered, but his certificate was still in date. He'd re-qualified just days before he was told he was to be made redundant. He'd not used his skills since, not any of them.

To his relief Harry saw that the red sticky stuff was jam. Sugar free strawberry jam to be precise. That gave him a clue as to why his neighbour was unresponsive. He strongly suspected she was diabetic and her blood sugar levels had either peaked or crashed. As he wasn't sure which he didn't attempt any treatment – he knew that in medical emergencies doing the wrong thing was often worse than doing nothing.

From the way she was positioned, it seemed clear she'd passed out in the chair whilst preparing a meal. He ran his fingers gently over her skull, which rested against a table leg, finding nothing to worry him. He pushed the chair away and quickly checked her arms and legs. Nothing seemed amiss and as she'd not fallen far it seemed unlikely she'd have sustained injuries. As long as it was her breakfast she'd been making, not last night's tea, she'd be fine once the ambulance crew gave her fluids and whatever else she needed. Her pulse was a bit on the fast side, but strong. "I'm just going to put you into the recovery position, to help you breathe more easily."

Once he'd done that Harry, knowing the medics would appreciate as much information as he could provide, found her handbag and the insulin in her bathroom cupboard.

"You're going to be just fine, Claire," he told her. "Ah, here's the ambulance."

Two hours later a young woman entered the kitchen via the house rather than the back door and demanded to know who he was and what he was doing.

"I'm Harry and I'm cleaning up the mess Claire and I made between us. Now I'll ask you the same question."

"I'm Lisa, Claire's daughter. And you're the neighbour who found Mum and got help. Sorry I snapped…"

Harry waved away her attempts at an apology. He knew how easy it was to take out your own worries on a person, or animal, who'd not meant any harm but just happened to be there.

"I've come to feed the cat and fetch some clothes," Lisa said. "What mess? Everything looks fine."

Harry explained about Claire spilling jam and him smashing a pane of glass to get to her.

"And you've replaced it already?"

"I'm a builder," he told her. "Now, you get back to your mum. Don't worry about the cat – I found his food when I was looking for a cleaning cloth and filled his bowl."

"Thanks, Harry. Thanks for everything."

She left him with her copy of her mum's key, and the promise to call in and let him know how Claire was doing.

When Lisa had gone, Harry smiled to himself. "I'm a builder," he'd told her. He was. He'd been made redundant, but that didn't make him useless. As he'd repaired the door he'd realised that. For a time the loss of his job had caused him to slip into depression, just as lack of blood sugar had caused Claire to slip into a coma. Doctors were treating Claire. If needs be he'd ask one to treat him too.

"But I think maybe I'm already on the road to recovery," he said as he stroked the cat.

21. Room To Grow

Janet did congratulate me on my engagement, but she didn't do so with much enthusiasm. Most other people thought avoiding the shame of being an unmarried mother was the most important thing, but not her.

"They're sending a man to the moon, Prue. Don't you think it's time people got over being shocked about something that's been happening for centuries?"

I agreed with her, but I needed somewhere to live and didn't want to raise a baby on my own. My parents wouldn't have kicked me out, but they made it clear they considered marrying the baby's father was the right thing to do. Besides, I loved Paul.

"Are you sure you'll be happy in a flat, surrounded by nothing but concrete?" Janet asked.

If anyone else had expressed such doubts, I'd have reminded them how awful last winter's big freeze was and say how nice it would be living in a warm, modern flat with an inside lav and hot water at the turn of a tap. "I'm going up in the world by becoming a city girl," I might have replied gaily. I didn't, not to the friend who knew me so well. With her, I went on the defensive.

"You calling me a snob?" She wasn't, but I didn't want to be told my new home wouldn't suit me.

"No. You're not a snob, Prue. You're just used to something so different."

"Yes, I am. Soil under my fingernails, never wearing anything new or owning anything I don't need to survive."

I'd grown up on what we called a farm, but was really a smallholding. Our house was huge, old and draughty. The roof leaked whenever the wind came from one direction and fires smoked when it switched round. I'd loved the space and the freedom; there was room for friends to play, or later dance, with no worries about breaking anything precious. Being poor never seemed to matter. Maybe my siblings and I were so different from other kids our lack of trendy clothes and money to spend on records didn't count. We always had fresh veg, fruit, milk and eggs. Sometimes there was a surplus to trade with neighbours and storekeepers for whatever we needed and couldn't produce ourselves.

Janet's dad went out to work. Her mum didn't make clothes; she bought them and washed them in a machine. She bought food too. Not just things like flour and sugar, but bread baked and sliced ready to eat! Janet's chores were easy things in the house, not earthing up row after row of spuds, or pruning prickly gooseberry bushes. When I went there, I loved vacuuming the brightly coloured carpets, such a change from beating rugs on the line. Even so, Janet usually suggested coming to ours, except when we wanted to watch television.

Seeing it through her eyes helped me appreciate the big flower and herb filled garden. When we worked out how old milk was when delivered to her doorstep, I almost felt good taking my turn milking Clementine our Jersey cow. I never had to be persuaded of the virtues of picking sun-ripened strawberries, digging the sweetest, crunchiest carrots or popping peas straight from the pod into my mouth. I felt so proud when our family sat down to eat a meal, most of which I'd helped grow from seed.

Then I met Paul and different things mattered more. I resented not being able to buy myself a lipstick, or have someone other than Mum trim my hair. I looked into the future and saw life would be different. As one of four children, including a boy, the smallholding I'd always considered home would never be mine. Just as, through Janet, I'd seen the advantages of the farm, through Paul I saw the benefits of something different.

Paul seemed so rich nothing was out of his reach. If I exclaimed over something pretty in a shop window, he'd buy it for me.

"I want my girl to have nice things," he said.

"Am I your girl, then?"

"Of course you are, Prue."

I felt warm inside when he said that. He'd not talked of love or a future together, but the way he spoke made me think those things would come.

If I was hungry when he came round after work, we went to the chippy and he got me a hot meal right away; no peeling potatoes and waiting for the fat to heat with him. Not everything was instant, but it still seemed miraculous when, come summer, he took me on his work's trip to the seaside. At first maybe all that turned my head a little, but I cared for him as much as the things he bought me. By the time I realised he wasn't rich at all, I knew I loved him anyway.

Within minutes of me telling him I was pregnant, he'd proposed. Sort of. "We'll get married as soon as we can," was how he put it. He promised to be a good father and husband. Talked of the council flat we'd rent, near to where he worked, and the TV and washing machine he'd get us on HP.

"I'll get to vacuum my own carpets whenever I like," I told Janet, as part of the conversation in which I tried to convince her, and myself, that I was looking forward to living such a life.

She smiled then. "That's true. I suppose because we were at yours so often, and I loved it there, I find it difficult to think of you somewhere so different. If it's what you want, then I'm happy for you."

"And you'll be my bridesmaid?" I patted my belly. "And godmother?"

"Of course!"

We talked about my dress and flowers and how I'd have my hair. I worked hard at not worrying that Paul and I didn't have enough in common and that he didn't really know me.

The wedding was quickly arranged and the church hall booked for afterwards. Friends and neighbours offered to make plates of food for the reception and I knew they'd wear their best clothes. They did the same for funerals and there was less notice for those. Not that I was really comparing my wedding day to such a sad occasion. I loved Paul and wanted to spend the rest of my life with him. I loved my unborn child too and wanted what was best for him or her. Two loving parents and a stable home would provide that. The baby wouldn't miss the freedom of the little farm as it would never know the difference. It wouldn't mind not planting seeds and waiting eagerly for them to sprout.

"Not bringing him to see his grandparents then?" Mum asked when I mentioned that.

"Of course I will."

"Soon as he's big enough, we'll make him his own little garden, just as we did for you."

I had to hold back tears. That garden was mine no more. Of course I was always going to have to give it up and move away, so why was I so upset?

No wonder Paul didn't understand me. I hadn't myself until then. I'd told myself it was his love for me I doubted and used that to mask the fact that I'd never have a patch of earth that was truly mine.

"What's wrong, Prue love?" Mum asked.

"Just wedding nerves," I assured her, hoping it was true.

The night before my wedding I was restless and went to check the village hall. There were flowers everywhere, many grown by me, and a huge pile of gifts. One looked like a broom, another could be dress making scissors, a wrinkly package felt like washing up gloves. It was good that they were so practical and it was just as generous of our family and friends to provide what we needed as it would have been to give us things we merely wanted.

The door creaked open and Paul came in. "Oh dear, you're not going to get any surprises."

"It's OK, I've not properly looked and I don't really know what any of them are."

"Really? Isn't it obvious?"

"No. Most are in boxes," I pointed out. "And that one looks like a watering can. No one would give us a watering can, would they?"

"They might." He looked uncomfortable.

I checked the label. "It's from my brother."

"He knows you like growing plants."

"Exactly and he knows I won't be able to now. He wouldn't be so cruel as to remind me of what I can't have!" I hadn't meant to snap, to reveal the truth that until so recently I'd kept to myself.

"No, of course he wouldn't." Paul pulled me close. "And I wouldn't be so cruel as to give you a life where you couldn't do what's important to you."

"What do you mean? You're not going to marry me?"

"Silly girl." He handed me a tiny package. "Your wedding present."

I felt it. "Keys?"

"For plot eighteen on the allotment site. I know you won't technically own it, but it's as good as. Just like our flat, there's a contract with the council, but for the allotment it just says Mrs Marten not Mr and Mrs. I'll help with the heavy stuff, especially while you're pregnant, but it'll be all yours."

I wanted to thank him, tell him I loved him, kiss him. Instead I mumbled, "Two keys?"

"One for the gate to the site, one for the shed to keep that lot in." He gestured to our gifts.

So it really was a watering can? What I'd thought was a broom was probably a rake, the scissors might be secateurs. "You've definitely given away the surprise now, but I'm glad you did."

"You'll probably be glad I'm spoiling the other one too. Least, your mum said you would."

"Another surprise?"

"We're going on honeymoon. Just a few days, but you'll need to pack and your mum thought doing that tonight would be a good way of helping with your wedding nerves. All brides get them she told me."

"She's right."

"You've been having doubts?"

"I did, but I don't now. And a honeymoon will be lovely, thank you. Where are we going?"

"I want to keep at least one surprise, so I'll tell you tomorrow."

Paul didn't get to do that. His boss made a speech and revealed the reason Paul first came to work for him; the annual summer outing. "Paul wanted to take this new girl he'd met. Frankly I didn't expect either his employment or the relationship to last long, but he's proved me wrong on both counts. He's a real asset to the company and I'm glad we can do something for the happy couple by providing a few days honeymoon in Bournemouth."

"You really took the job, just so I could see the sea six months later?" I asked Paul.

"Not just that. Any job would have meant I was able to give you the things you wanted then, but I wanted somewhere with good prospects, so I could give you what you needed for the rest of our lives."

"You were thinking of marriage, even then?"

"Prue, almost since the day I met you, I've been hoping for this." He led me onto the floor, for our first dance as man and wife.

"Mum said you must be a planner, as there's a waiting list for allotments."

"Not so much a planner; more of an optimist. A friend of my dad's runs the site, so I asked him to put your name down right after we cycled to the river that day and it rained. Do you remember?"

Of course I did. It was the day we first kissed. The rain had started as we cycled home, a brief but heavy shower. I'd not even noticed I was soaked until we reached home.

I did notice the rice our wedding guests showered us with!

As Janet hugged me, just before we went away on honeymoon, I finally answered her question. "Yes, I'm sure I'll be happy in the flat. It might be surrounded by concrete, but it's just a short walk to where I'll have a patch of garden of my own. And even more importantly, it's a short walk back to the man who loves me as much as I love him."

22. Ginny's Restoration

Although there were three of us, it hadn't felt that way as we viewed the house. I'd politely followed the estate agent into room after room with Ginny, my wife, dutifully following me. She was there physically, but I knew Ginny was thinking of another place and time.

The estate agent had made much of the conservatory and the fact it had once been featured in one of those glossy lifestyle magazines. At last we'd seen everywhere else.

"And here is the conservatory!" the estate agent pushed open the doors and gestured us inside rather theatrically.

I was thoroughly underwhelmed. The once white paint was missing more than it was there. Some of whatever covering had last been on the floor still adhered to the concrete base. Dusty blinds blocked the light, and a few plastic pots and dessicated plants huddled in corners. To be fair, it was a good size, but I'd expected that. The estate agent had built my expectations too high by acting as though he'd been saving the best to last.

He looked at us expectantly. I keep saying he, because although the man had introduced himself, with what sounded like two first names, I couldn't remember either of them. Craig David? No, that wasn't right.

Once my initial feeling of slight anti-climax had worn off I saw the conservatory was nicely proportioned. Enough peeling paint and paper remained to prove it hadn't always been neglected. Different colours and patterns showed in various spots. Lots and lots of them, particularly along the long wall of the house, against which it was attached. For anyone with an interest in interior design, as Ginny and I once had, it could be a lot of fun gradually removing it all and looking at the choices of previous owners. Actually it was quite difficult for me to resist tugging gently on a particularly tempting strip of wallpaper.

"I'd like to show you this," said the estate agent. Ricky Martin, was it? No, maybe not. He handed me a large, slippery, clear plastic wallet containing a page torn from a glossy magazine, featuring a fabulous conservatory.

The similarity of structure was obvious but it took Mark Anthony pointing out the flakes of white paint and distinctive window attachments to convince me that elegant illustration was a photo of the room in which I stood.

"Lovely wasn't it?" the estate agent prompted.

I nodded to agree that it had indeed looked very nice and then again to show I believed it could be again. It would take more than the 'just a little work' he claimed, but it could indeed be made lovely. That didn't seem to matter much. We'd looked at some houses which were already lovely and some which were dreadful and probably always would be. Other than to quietly say she didn't want to live there, Ginny didn't express much of an opinion about any of them.

The conservatory was different. She didn't immediately follow us, but stood in the doorway for a few moments, looking in. I really did think she was looking at what was before her, not just into herself, her memories.

George Michael, or whoever he was, moved toward her, magazine illustration to the ready. I put a hand on his arm and shook my head. He shrugged and fiddled with the blinds, then with a sound of triumph he pulled them open and flooded the room with light. That somehow made it look better and worse at the same time.

I thought I heard an exclamation from Ginny.

"Was that a good 'oh' or a bad one?" Jack Niklaus wondered aloud.

It wasn't until he asked that I knew for sure it wasn't wishful thinking and Ginny really had responded, with feeling, to seeing the conservatory brought out of the gloom. She'd been so subdued since the fire. Shock probably, combined with sadness over what we'd lost. I understood – I'd felt the same myself. It was so hard to take in the fact that the place we'd scrimped and done without to buy, and which for years we'd worked on to get exactly how we wanted it, was now gone.

The fire had started in the dining room and seemed to be contained, so we'd rescued our photo albums and a few other irreplaceable items, before the fire brigade arrived and stopped us going back – very wisely I'm sure. Although the damage wasn't widespread, it was enough to make the house unsafe and it had to come down.

Most of the things we lost could easily be bought again, or replaced with something similar, once we had somewhere to put them. The children and their families had been safe in their own homes when it happened. The smoke alarm had done its job brilliantly. We'd escaped without injury and still had our memories and each other. There was much to be thankful for.

The insurance policy provided two options. We could have the house rebuilt, as close as possible to how it had been, or we could accept the estimated cost of that and do our own thing. Neither of us could face starting again with even less than the shell we'd mortgaged when we first married. I wanted to buy somewhere else. Ginny didn't object. While the insurance and everything was being sorted out we rented a place.

If you hadn't known her before you'd have thought Ginny was fine, but to me it was as though she was a watered down version of herself. She phoned the kids and asked about their lives, but she didn't tease them or shriek with laughter. She put her blouse on the right way round and buttoned it correctly, but it was just any blouse – not one specially selected to suit the season and go well with her skirt or trousers. She served meals on time, but it might be a piece of fish accompanied by potatoes, cauliflower and white sauce. It wasn't burned or raw or anything, but it was clearly just food to her. Oh, it's hard to explain. Until the fire she'd always been so vibrant, so animated, so interested in everything.

We'd given up our business, as decorators of other people's homes, two years previously. It had seemed sensible to stop in our sixties and enjoy an active retirement. That's how everyone else saw it – retiring from a job of work. It wasn't though. That had been our passion, and although we'd acknowledged that as we got older we wouldn't be so keen to do all the practical things ourselves, we'd planned to carry on as advisors and designers. I couldn't do it without Ginny, or I certainly didn't want to. It seemed she didn't really want to do anything at all. I don't mean she'd got lazy, she'd just lost all her enthusiasm. Her spirit.

I wouldn't have minded if she'd hated the conservatory. Such a strong reaction would have been so much better than the way she'd just been going along with whatever I suggested. I hoped though that she'd love it – because by then I did. The work which needed doing was all things we could do. It was exactly the kind of project we used to love. Actually it was the kind of thing I missed since we'd got our house perfect, and I know she'd started to feel the same way before the fire.

Ginny walked into the conservatory and gestured for Ray Charles to give her the magazine page.

She studied the image for quite some time. "It is nice," she said. "But I think a touch more colour would lift it."

With those words I knew my wonderful wife was on her way back.

The sale went through quite quickly and as each piece of paper was signed, each part of the process completed, Ginny became more and more like her real self. Soon we moved in and set to work making the house nice. Not just nice, but exactly as we wanted it.

We got in professionals to do all the work on the kitchen and bathroom, but we were very precise in what we wanted – eventually. As we had before with our old house, we considered almost every possibility, bouncing ideas off each other and discussing and dissecting until we were sure. The bedrooms, hallway, stairs and landing we mostly tackled ourselves. We went for warm, cheerful earth tones – oranges and browns, terracotta red and sandy yellow. Ginny and I spent hours in shops and markets, at auctions and exhibitions, getting just the right furniture and accessories. We didn't rush at all, but we worked quite quickly. Years of that sort of thinking made our thought processes rapid and the actual work quicker still.

Just as the estate agent had done, we saved the conservatory until last. I told Ginny my thoughts on uncovering the past, layer by layer. We'd taken to eating out there. Perhaps that was because we still had the photo James

Dean had given us, and that showed the room set up for a dinner party.

"Who?" Ginny asked when I mentioned him.

"The estate agent."

"He was no James Dean, not even a Bob Dylan."

"I may have got it wrong. Daniel Craig?"

"Definitely not, I'd have remembered that!"

Recalling her enthusiasm for Bond movies I decided to change the subject. "We can use another room to eat in while we work in here."

"Yes, but one last dinner first."

Ginny served up another of those all white fish and cauliflower dinners. This time it was deliberate. A joke, sort of. She'd recreated that photo as well as she could – white roses in a white vase, white linen cloth and napkins. It all looked very elegant but, as she'd said the first time, it needed more colour.

"Don't worry, we're going to get it," she assured me.

She was right. Every few days we'd carefully go down a layer and each time we'd bring back the dining table and chairs, and Ginny would create an appropriate meal to surprise me.

We guessed the nineties were the last time the conservatory was decorated, so we had Thai food after the initial clear up. It's a favourite of ours and that's the decade we first discovered it.

We found a lot of pastel mauve we thought must have been applied during the eighties.

"You know, I'm sure our bathroom was once this exact shade," Ginny said as we celebrated uncovering it with a quiche Lorraine and Arctic Roll.

The rather intense seventies patterns were matched with Spaghetti Bolognaise and a bottle of Mateus Rose followed by a Black Forest Gateau. We laughed together over memories of serving such food to guests and feeling sophisticated.

"Maybe we really were?" Ginny suggested. "Foreign food was still quite unusual then, and so was wine with dinner."

"You're right. It's easy to forget how different some things used to be. However did we survive with only three TV channels and no mobile phone?"

When we uncovered the psychedelic swirls of the sixties, Ginny created a 'hedgehog', from things on sticks stuck into a grapefruit. That was an appetizer to go with a glass of Blue Nun. The main course was a Vesta curry, made from a kit.

"I discovered you can still buy them, but I'm sure they've changed the recipe," Ginny said. "This tastes a lot more like a proper curry than I remember."

I tried a forkful and agreed it wasn't the same as I recalled from my childhood. "Probably for the best."

"I suppose so, but somehow it's less exciting. I remember Mum announcing days ahead that we'd be trying a new kind of food for our tea and then us sitting round the table waiting to see who would be first to taste it."

At last we got down to the plain plaster in its usual pinky orange shade. We had baked beans on toast for supper — something we'd often eaten all those years ago when we started out.

"Which style did you like best?' Ginny asked.

"The first one," I told her without hesitation. Not just because of how it looked, but because it was that which had brought my wife back to me.

"Like in the magazine?" she asked.

I nodded.

"Me too, but with a bit of a twist." She wouldn't tell me what that was, but there was a sparkle in her eyes so it was sure to be fine with me.

"Dean Martin would be proud," I said once it was all cool, pristine and elegant white.

"If you mean that estate agent, I think his name was Bruce Lee. Let's find out by asking him round. I'm sure he'd like to see what we've done."

Ginny worked on her little twist in secret. When she'd finished, the conservatory was still mostly white, but it didn't seem that way – just as an all grey sky doesn't seem dull when lit by a rainbow. There were hints of colour everywhere. The tablecloth was white still, but at each of the six settings was a napkin in red, orange or yellow. The chairs were covered to match. The white curtains were tied back with emerald sashes. The flowers in the little white vases were vibrant pinks and purple. The monochrome prints on the walls had cornflower blue frames. It was magical.

The estate agent was suitably impressed. "Better even than the illustration I showed you!"

"Thanks, Hugh," I said.

"His name isn't Hugh Grant, it's Billy Joel," Ginny corrected me.

"Actually it's Peter Gabriel."

We both apologised.

"It's fine, lots of people get it wrong."

Although he smiled as he said it, somehow it made me feel worse. Thankfully Ginny had something else to show us, so there was no awkward silence.

Her rainbow decor was cleverer than I'd realised. She'd made complete sets of the napkins, chair covers and pretty much everything else in each of the key colours she'd selected. In just a few moments the room could be transformed into sunshine yellow, cool blue, exciting red…

Peter the estate agent was overtaken by whatever emotion it is that's considerably beyond impressed. "You can call me Greg Norman or anything else you like if you'll agree to work for me," he said.

"Thank you, Peter," Ginny replied doubtfully. "But I don't know anything about selling houses." I saw her looking for a polite way to say she had no interest in learning.

"I didn't mean that, at least not directly. I was hoping you'd agree to advise my clients on how to decorate their homes prior to sale, and offer the same service to purchasers afterwards. For a suitable fee, of course."

"We'd be delighted!" Ginny told him, even before he'd got the last sentence out. "Well, I would. How about you, love?"

"I'm delighted too." Of course I was – I had my wonderful wife back. As a bonus, we'd get to continue with the kind of work which had meant so much to us.

23. Trusting Love Will Blossom

The florist shop door opened, making the little bell ring cheerfully. Nicole glanced up from the arrangement she was assembling, ready to give a beaming smile and cheery greeting. No words came, because he was back. The gorgeous man she'd admired until she discovered the truth. He was a blatant, and totally unrepentant love rat!

She probably did smile; despite knowing that emotionally speaking he wasn't to be trusted, his presence made it hard for her to behave rationally. Nicole concentrated on the lady customer in front of her in an attempt to avoid gazing into the man's sky blue eyes. If she caught even a glimpse of his kissable lips curving into a lopsided grin, her knees would threaten to give way. She must not fall for his charm again, not now she knew he was a cheat.

The first time he came in he'd said, "I'd like a mix of really cheerful colours in blooms which will last well. And scented, if that's OK?"

His smile made her want to say he could have absolutely anything. Fortunately the way he looked at her interfered with her breathing so much she couldn't speak and so avoided blurting out anything inappropriate. He'd stayed for a while, making conversation easy by talking about some kind of show in the church hall and asking about different flowers whenever she was free of customers.

Nicole desperately hoped the bouquet was for his mother or sister. Him asking, "Do you have plans for lunch?" as he finally put his chosen flowers on the counter seemed to confirm that he was single.

As she was trying to pull herself together to reply he'd selected a small card and written 'to my Jane, from your Charles.' Not for his mum then!

"I hope your sister enjoys them."

He'd looked surprised. "I don't have a sister."

"I do and I'm having lunch with her!" She put as much indignation into her voice as she could. Did this Charles really think she'd agree to a date with him knowing he was involved with another girl?

"Oh. Right. Another time?" Yes, it seemed he did think exactly that.

"I don't think so," Nicole had said, quite firmly.

"Sorry, I didn't mean to offend you, but surely you can't blame a guy for trying?"

She did, but kept the thought to herself. It wasn't professional to be rude to customers and she doubted he'd mend his ways just because she disapproved.

Nicole had known such men existed. She'd learned the hard way and vowed never to date a man unless she had absolute proof she could trust him. Unfortunately that didn't leave her many options and she'd been single for a while.

Just as it was unusual to be certain a man could be trusted, it was rare to know he couldn't – at least in time to avoid getting hurt. Charles was a real exception there.

"Maybe I should be grateful he didn't try to hide his cheating and let me see what he was really like before I started to care about him?" she'd said to her sister.

Madison had married someone who, as far as Nicole could tell, was honest and faithful. She certainly hoped so, both for sister's sake and because she craved proof such men existed.

"There are far more good men than bad," Madison had said. "Try to be a little more trusting,"

Nicole followed this advice when the man with sky blue eyes returned to the florist shop three months later.

"Hello again," he'd said giving the adorable grin she remembered. "I don't think I made a very good impression last time. Can I try again?"

Nicole had nodded. Maybe he'd split up from his girlfriend and learned his lesson?

"I'm Bradley," he'd held out a hand.

"Bradley?" He'd signed 'Charles' before.

"That's right. Bradley Wilson."

"Oh!" So he didn't sign the card on his own behalf. Madison had been right, Nicole should be more trusting. If she had, maybe she'd have guessed he'd been buying flowers on behalf of someone else. As Bradley's warm fingers wrapped gently around hers, Nicole felt that jolt of electricity she'd read about but never experienced. Again he stayed for a time, chatting as he chose flowers.

"There's a new Italian restaurant next door, I see," he said.

Nicole mumbled something about pizza.

"That's my favourite too. Will you let me buy you one tonight?"

Nicole was trying to say yes when he picked out a card and wrote, 'for my Beatrice, from your Benedict'.

Surely he couldn't have two friends who'd ask him to buy flowers and use the same wording on the card? She'd been right not to trust him!

"Where shall I pick you up tonight?" he asked after paying.

"You can't."

"Another time?"

"NO!"

He'd left, looking disappointed and slightly confused.

Nicole told herself she'd had a lucky escape and no interest in the man, right until she saw him waiting patiently until she was free to serve him. Again she found it hard to speak properly, smiled just at the pleasure of being near him.

"I'm hoping it's third time lucky," he said as he placed his flowers on the counter. "Will you come for a pizza, or even just a drink the next time you're free?"

He seemed so genuine Nicole wanted to say yes immediately, but when he signed the card, 'to my Rosalind, from your Orlando' she had something completely different to say. "You can't keep playing with people like this!"

He frowned for a moment and then laughed. "I'm not playing with people – I'm in plays with them. I belong to an amateur dramatic group. Giving flowers to our opposite numbers is a tradition. As Charles in Blythe Spirit I gave them to Jane, and during Much Ado About Nothing Benedict bought them for Beatrice. I never thought to explain as, whenever I come in here, you're the only woman I'm thinking about."

Nicole couldn't think how to apologise for her suspicions, but Bradley could. "Come out with me tonight, please?"

She still had no absolute proof he'd never hurt her, and never would have, but at last she had regained her trust enough to take the chance of happiness. "Thank you, I'd like that."

24. Gift For A Lifetime

Barbara's son pulled yet another gift out from under his brightly decorated tree. "This one's for you, Therona."

The girl was ten and although not quite the youngest, she was Barbara's newest grandchild. Step-grandchild really, but that was too much of a mouthful. She was a beautiful child with her mother's dark hair, huge eyes and exotic complexion.

Therona flicked over the tag to read who was responsible for the gift. "From everyone?" she asked, sounding puzzled.

Barbara always enjoyed watching her grandchildren unwrap their gifts, but especially so when it was a big item several people had clubbed together to buy. There had already been two of them that year – a laptop and smartphone respectively for the two oldest boys. They'd each had to say which model they wanted which spoiled the surprise, but they were clearly pleased to get exactly what they'd hoped for.

Therona however was unaware that she was getting the new bike she so wanted. She was using a hand me down that was a little small for her and made strange rattles if she got up any speed. The size of the package she'd been handed wasn't much of a clue, as it contained only a purple safety helmet and another tiny box.

"Thank you. It's my favourite colour," she said as she tried on the helmet. "It fits too."

"Open the other box!" her stepbrother urged.

Therona did, and extracted a rusty key. "I don't understand."

"It's for the shed. Come on!"

Barbara didn't join the rush to the shed in her son's garden, as with so many people ahead of her she wouldn't see Therona's reaction. Instead she stayed in the warm, waiting for her children and grandchildren to return. Until a couple of years ago Barbara would have gone into the kitchen and basted the turkey or spooned cranberry sauce into a serving dish, but she didn't have that kind of relationship with her new daughter-in-law. By the time Barbara realised she had nothing to do but wait, and might seem stand offish for not joining the others, it was too late. She smiled as she heard Therona's delighted squeal and the murmur of voices assuring her that the bike really was just for her.

After that excitement there weren't many more gifts to be exchanged. Two were from Barbara. One was a lacy top she'd crocheted for Therona's mum. After noticing she owned several in a similar style and was fond of the colour turquoise it had seemed the ideal gift. It had been a lot of work, but Barbara hadn't minded. In a way it had felt like a kind of penance for the cool reception Barbara had given to her son's second wife. It wasn't the woman's fault his first marriage had broken down, but her and Therona moving in had put paid to all hope that it could be salvaged.

She unfolded the top. "Oh! It's lovely. Thank you so much." She became almost tearful when she realised Barbara had made it herself.

Usually Barbara's gifts got a more modest response. That was in keeping with the gifts themselves. She had a lot of family to buy for and often chose practical items.

She knew her gift to Therona wouldn't get a delighted squeal, nor the emotional reaction displayed by her mother.

Therona unwrapped the flower pot, pack of seeds, label and tiny bag of compost. It was something Barbara had given to each of her grandchildren when she thought they were old enough. That was usually about five for the girls, a little later for the boys. She tried to catch them while they were still interested in everything but old enough that, with a little supervision, they could do the seed sowing and later care themselves. That way they learned and remembered the experience.

Over the years each of Barbara's children and then grandchildren had been given all they needed to grow appropriate plants. Mustard and cress suited those children who'd shown little interest in gardening, as it was indoors and very quick to produce a tasty result. As there was lots of seed in each pack repeat sowings could be made, which no doubt helped teach them valuable lessons about forward planning. For similar reasons some of the boys had been given fiery radish seeds. Huge sunflowers were a good choice to boost the confidence of more reserved children, as the results were so impressive.

Nasturtiums were what Barbara herself had been given, many years ago. She'd politely thanked her grandad but hadn't exactly been waiting eagerly for the chance to sow the seeds. When the first one germinated she'd surprised herself by feeling both proud and a little excited.

Since then Barbara had developed a real passion for gardening which had given her years of pleasure, as well as lots of fresh fruit, vegetables and exercise. She was now immensely grateful to her grandad and wished to give her own grandchildren the same good start in life. Gardening kept her healthy and optimistic and although she still did almost everything herself it was a friendly sort of occupation. There were clubs to join and events to attend for those who wished. Passers by stopped to take a look and exchange a few words and some local people even exchanged plants. Neighbours received bunches of flowers and fresh produce, in return they gave her lifts to the shop, or collected bulky bags of compost or helped with heavy jobs.

Barbara had thought long and hard over which seeds to give Therona. She was old enough to handle fiddly seeds and to have the patience to look after something slow growing, so some of the usual restrictions didn't apply. Despite seeming a bit reserved the child, like her mother, favoured bright colours, so flowers seemed right.

After considering various options, Barbara had bought nasturtiums. Quick, impressive results were appreciated at any age and however experienced the gardener. Barbara still grew them herself, trying out the new colours and forms which came on the market each year. She'd grown mini nasturtiums in pastel shades, climbers in glowing copper and bronze, those with attractively marbled foliage. For Therona she selected a mixture which had the best of these qualities – climbers in bright shades for impact and all with the colourful foliage which would make them interesting even before blooms developed.

"Thank you," Therona said politely after unwrapping her gift.

Barbara wasn't the slightest bit disappointed with that response. As with sowing seeds the real reward would come later, when she learned Therona had planted them and enjoyed watching them grow. As she lived nearby maybe

Barbara would be really lucky and she'd get to help with the planting or watering and so be able to pass on her knowledge directly – but if not that wouldn't matter as her son would help his stepdaughter.

After a truly superb lunch everyone went for a lap or two of the local park. Or five or six in the case of Therona and everyone else with a bicycle. There was a lot of laughter and messing about on play equipment as the grandson who'd been given the smart phone used it to take photos of everyone. Barbara was persuaded to stand in front of a climbing frame with various family members behind her.

"That's wonderful!" she said when she saw the result. It appeared that her family had formed an upside down human pyramid, balanced on her shoulders.

"I'll print you one out, Granny," the boy promised.

A sudden sleety shower had everyone scurrying back inside. Barbara went up to her son's guest room to check her hair hadn't become too much of a fright, and to remove the extra sweater she'd put on before going out.

When she came back downstairs Barbara was surprised to see Therona alone in the living room. The child was holding her pack of nasturtium seeds and had tears trickling down her face. Barbara wondered if she'd made a terrible mistake and should have just bought the girl a gift voucher.

"Hey, what's brought this on?" Barbara asked, wiping away the child's tears with a tissue.

"I was talking to the others… my new cousins… and said it seemed like an odd gift. They explained that it wasn't, not from you. That you did the same for every one of your grandchildren."

"That's true. I don't quite understand…"

"No, you don't do you? You don't see why I'm surprised that you've done the same for me?"

Barbara didn't, not immediately, but gradually saw what she was getting at. "It shows I consider you one of the family? Well, of course I do!"

"Granny!" Therona said and hugged her.

That was the first time those things had happened – both using the term and the spontaneous show of affection. It was a moment Barbara would treasure, but she was also looking forward to watching those plants, and that dear child, grow.

Thank you for reading this book. I hope you enjoyed it. If you did, I'd really appreciate a short review on Amazon, Goodreads – or anywhere else.

The author can be found at www.patsycollins.co.uk You may like to sign up for my newsletter and get a free story, plus news of the latest releases, special offers and behind the scenes insights. There's a link on the website, or you can use subscribepage.io/ItLSNa

More Books by Patsy Collins

Novels

Firestarter
Escape To The Country
A Year And A Day
Paint Me A Picture
Leave Nothing But Footprints
Acting Like A Killer

Little Mallow cosy mystery series

Disguised Murder and Community Spirit in Little Mallow
Dependable Friends and Deceitful Neighbours
in Little Mallow
Deadly Words and Innocent Gossip in Little Mallow

Non-fiction

From Story Idea To Reader
(co-written with Rosemary J. Kind)

A Year Of Ideas:
365 sets of writing prompts and exercises

Short story collections

Criminal Intent
Crime In Mind

Over The Garden Fence
Up The Garden Path
Through The Garden Gate
In The Garden Air

No Family Secrets
Can't Choose Your Family
Keep It In The Family
Family Feeling
Happy Families

All That Love Stuff
With Love And Kisses
Lots Of Love
Love Is The Answer

Slightly Spooky Stories I
Slightly Spooky Stories II
Slightly Spooky Stories III
Slightly Spooky Stories IV
Slightly Spooky Stories V

Just A Job
Perfect Timing
A Way With Words
Dressed To Impress
Coffee & Cake
Making A Move
Days To Remember
Not A Drop To Drink

www.ingramcontent.com/pod-product-compliance
Lightning Source LLC
Chambersburg PA
CBHW070500170726
48291CB00008B/2578